BUCHANAN'S
BIG FIGHT

Fawcett Gold Medal Books
by Jonas Ward:

☐ BUCHANAN CALLS THE SHOTS   14210 $1.75

☐ BUCHANAN GETS MAD   14209 $1.75

☐ BUCHANAN'S MANHUNT   14119 $1.75

☐ BUCHANAN'S RANGE WAR   14357 $1.75

☐ BUCHANAN'S REVENGE   14179 $1.75

☐ BUCHANAN'S STOLEN RAILWAY   13977 $1.75

☐ BUCHANAN'S TEXAS TREASURE   14175 $1.75

☐ GET BUCHANAN!   14062 $1.50

☐ THE NAME'S BUCHANAN   14135 $1.75

☐ TRAP FOR BUCHANAN   14082 $1.50

BUCHANAN'S BIG FIGHT

by

Jonas Ward

FAWCETT GOLD MEDAL • NEW YORK

BUCHANAN'S BIG FIGHT

Copyright © 1981 William R. Cox

Published by Fawcett Gold Medal Books, a unit of CBS Publications, the Consumer Publishing Division of CBS Inc.

ISBN: 0-449-14406-2

Printed in the United States of America

First Fawcett Gold Medal printing: May 1981

10 9 8 7 6 5 4 3 2 1

BUCHANAN'S
BIG FIGHT

1.

Buchanan sat at a table in the Cheyenne Cattlemen's Club and looked at the draft for a thousand dollars which the stout man had placed before him.

He said, "I'm not truly Coco Bean's manager. I'm his friend and I work with him sometimes when he's in trainin'. But the money, that's his."

The stout man's name was Charlie Emory, known as Happy Charlie, promoter, broker, all-around operator, a man who exuded prosperity and jollity. He pushed the crisp piece of paper toward Coco and said, "Cash it before the train leaves for Denver. Make sure I'm on the level. In a few minutes you'll be meetin' royalty. Ain't that somethin'?"

Coco looked at Tom, waited. He was over six feet, his skin was ebony, his face round and displaying little evidence of his long career in the prize ring. He was the undefeated black champion of the world. One gnarled fist touched the paper.

"What you think, Tom?"

Buchanan leaned back. Sitting down, he towered over every other man in the room. He was six feet four, his shoulders were axe-handle wide. He had sandy hair and freckles. His green eyes were veiled at the moment, estimating the promoter. He asked, "You guaranteeing that Dan Ford will fight Coco in Denver?"

"Dan Ford beat Joe Goss. Now he's havin' trouble gettin' Paddy Ryan to meet him for the title. He needs money. We got the money. He's on a train from New York to Denver right now." Emory gestured with a fat cigar. He wore a diamond on his ring finger. His coat was of broadcloth, his striped trousers were sharply creased. He wore polished city boots and a corded gray vest. He was no more than forty but he was going bald. He smelled of a fancy barber shop.

Buchanan said, "We been huntin' and fishin' Wyoming for some time. Just found out Hayes is president." He flicked a newspaper with his finger. "Just heard about the Cutler cousins playin' Jesse James around the country. Thought we'd have some fun in Frisco for awhile. It's up to Coco. If he wants to go into trainin' and do all that work—well, it's up to him."

Coco said. "Fightin's my business. Never did hear of so much money for a bout."

"Ten thousand dollars, win, lose, or draw," said Emory. "Ten for each man, you bein' the western champion, him the foremost eastern challenger."

"Paddy Ryan won't fight Coco. No white champion will fight him."

"That's a good reason for you to take the money and go against Ford."

Buchanan thought of the side bets. He'd spent a lot of money in the past six months. He was never without funds but his Scottish ancestry made him conscious of the uncertainty of life for a frontiers-

8

man with no profession. He had been up and down the West since he was a boy, he knew all the dangers. He had been through bank failures and disastrous ventures in mining and ranching.

"It's up to Coco."

The black fighter picked up the draft. "If this here is good we'll be on the train."

"The parlor car," said Emory airily. "Sleeps a dozen people. Special to them that can afford it." He looked at the door to the club, stood up, expanding. "So, here comes the duke now."

A tall, thin man was making an entrance. At his heels, a burly individual and two women followed. The dozen denizens of the Cheyenne Club stared, choked on their drinks. Several arose in high indignation.

A rancher said loudly, "Hey, there. No women allowed!"

The group stopped dead, their chins lifted. They were all blue-eyed and blond. One of the women was plain but her bearing was regal. The other woman was rosy-cheeked, with her yellow hair pulled back in a knot, atop which perched a perky small hat. They wore riding clothes of a foreign cut, narrow polished boots. Buchanan came to his feet, trying to restrain himself from gazing at the younger woman.

Emory bustled forward in such haste that he tipped over his chair. "Gentlemen, gentlemen, please. These are distinguished visitors from our friends across the sea. This is—"

A rough voice cut him off. "No whores allowed this side of the tracks."

Emory gasped. "This is the Duke . . ."

Two men surged forward. Buchanan recognized Harve Jepson, one of the wealthy ranch owners of the countryside. With him was his foreman, another husky six-footer called Highpockets. "And who the hell are you, anyway, fat man?"

Buchanan said mildly. "Name of Emory. Guest of mine."

Jepson swiveled and stared at Buchanan. "You ain't from here. I know you, Buchanan. This here's a private club. You're out of order."

"Nice place you got here, too," said Buchanan. He looked around at the walls, the antler heads, the mirror stretching the length of the bar, the crystal chandelier, the hand-crafted tables and chairs. "Real nice."

"You damn right, and we mean to keep it that-away." Jepson had an unnaturally loud voice and a menacing manner. Several of the others present formed behind him.

"Uh-huh," said Buchanan. "Trouble is, you don't recognize ladies when you see them."

"I don't know these dudes and I ain't got any wish to know 'em. They can't come in this club."

Buchanan took a slow step forward. Emory was waving his arms, muttering, "The Duke and the Duchess . . ." Coco moved to stand slightly behind Buchanan. The newly arrived party seemed frozen in the doorway.

"They shouldn't stay in this club. They've been insulted. Before they leave, an apology is strictly in order."

"Apologize? You crazy or something, Buchanan?"

"No. I'm a charter member, case you don't recollect. Ain't been here in some time. You could look it up."

"I don't give a damn if you're President Rutherford B. Hayes. You can't run no rangdoodle in here."

Voices chimed in, alcoholic, agreeing. Emory plucked the bank draft from the table and staggered over to the astonished group at the door. "So sorry . . . Dumb cattle people . . . Please . . ."

The lean man and his lady backed away. The

burly man stood with his head lowered like a stubborn bull. The young blond girl did not budge.

Someone said, "Give it to 'em, Harve. Can't let 'em have a stinkin' inch, the whores."

Buchanan reached out. Negligently, he cuffed the ears of the one who had spoken. The man went backwards as though shot by a Colt .45.

Jepson howled, "Hey, you . . ."

Buchanan struck him alongside his head. Jepson went into the crowd. There was a wild yell and the bunch of them surged forward.

"Yep, a nice place. Too bad," said Buchanan.

Coco punched the first one, Buchanan the second. They moved a step apart, waiting. Each picked a man; their teamwork was perfect. Ranchers and their employees resembled nothing so much as flying tenpins. The bartender came with a heavy icebreaker, a sawed-off baseball bat. Buchanan took it away from him, tossed it. The mirror behind the bar splintered.

Coco picked up one of the more aggressive of the attackers, lifted him and tossed him. As he turned over in mid-air the man's feet slammed into the chandelier. Shards fell upon the struggling crowd.

The girl's voice said clearly, "Oh, nicely bowled."

Buchanan saw her out of the corner of his eye. She was well inside the room. Her blue eyes shone with pleasure. Her fists were clenched. He thought for a moment she was going to join the fray. Someone hit him with a bottle.

He said, "Enough is enough."

He began to punch. Beside him, Coco was dealing out punishment to anyone within reach. Booted feet kicked at them. They knocked down two men, seized another, used him as a shield, and retreated toward the door. There was a rule against guns in the club; Buchanan wondered if it was fully observed.

He said to the girl, "Ladies first. It's best we leave."

She said, "But you're doing so well."

"There's a town full of jaspers who might think different. If there's that private car I'd advise you and your people make for it."

Two men came at him. He threw the man he held, into them. Coco swung from right and left. Jepson had regained his feet. Buchanan grabbed him and hauled him away from the tumbling, bruised men of Cheyenne.

"Jepson, when you sober up you'll know you made a heap big mistake. These folks are special. A duke and a duchess. Can you get that in your thick head?"

With Buchanan's grasp choking him, Jepson managed to nod, his eyes bulging.

"You want trouble, you're liable to get it. From the governor, maybe the President of the United States. You understand?"

Jepson tried to speak, could not. His face was turning red.

Buchanan went on, "I'm takin' them out of here. They'll be with me. In my care."

Behind Jepson, Coco demolished two more of the combative cowmen. A chair crashed. A table was split.

Jepson choked out, "For gossake . . . take 'em outa here. . . . Anything. . . . Just get out before the joint comes apart."

"You do apologize?"

"I do. . . . Oh, sure I do!"

Buchanan released him. Jepson staggered back, caught the edge of the bar to maintain balance. One hand clawed at his throat, the other waved weakly.

Buchanan said to the blond girl, "You see? If you reason with 'em, they know how to behave."

Coco covered his back as he led her through the door and down the steps. The police station was beneath the club quarters. Officialdom was accustomed to the revelries of the cowmen, therefore somnolent as Emory hustled the four foreigners into the street. Buchanan, Coco, and the girl followed at a leisurely pace.

"Name's Buchanan. This is Coco Bean."

The girl said, "Caroline Lamb."

Emory whirled about. "*Lady* Caroline Lamb. Her brother, the Duke of Comberland. The Duchess of Comberland. And Brister, butler to the duke."

There was a Chinese restaurant on the corner. Buchanan waved a hand. "Best we should set awhile and get back our bearin's, don't you reckon?"

"Better to take out some food and go to the car," said Emory nervously. "Jepson is a rough customer."

"We haven't settled our business," Buchanan said. "We've got our gear and a couple of horses in town."

"Put the horses on the train," begged Emory. "Please. Here's the bank draft. I'm worried about our friends, here."

The Duke of Comberland spoke for the first time. His voice was soft and pleasant. "I say, no problem, y'know. Had I not seen how capable were our friends I should've been glad to take part up there. Brister, here, I had to hold him back. Fascinatin', the way you two go about it."

Buchanan said, "Coco is the black heavyweight champion of the world."

"Indeed, ah, yes, so Emory tells me. He's the one, then. I'm a devotee, y'know. Had the muffles on a few times myself." The duke smiled. "I do hope you're taking the bout in Denver."

"You're heading that way?"

"Had a hunt. Want to see some city life. They say Denver is wild and wooly."

"They could say that."

The duchess asked, "Wilder and woolier than the Cheyenne club?"

13

She had a nice smile. Buchanan looked at her, at the girl. Then he asked Coco, "You thought about it enough?"

"If I beat Ford, then Ford wins the championship—that makes me look pretty good, don't it? I know Ryan won't fight me. But I'd still feel good if I beat the man who beat him."

Buchanan said, "All right, Emory."

The stout man swiftly produced the bank draft. "There's just time to cash it. I'll have food brought to the car. You can't miss it. It'll be a great event. It'll set Denver on its ear. Hurry, now, hurry."

He was off, shepherding his charges toward the railway. Buchanan watched them go. The girl had a fine, natural long stride. She held herself like a lady, moved like a woman.

Coco said, "Lady Caroline Lamb. Woo-eee."

"Get to the bank," said Buchanan. "Nobody's takin' any real honest looks at a lady-anything."

"Oh-ho," said Coco. "You eyes buggin' out, Tom Buchanan. Purely buggin' out like a frog on a lily pad."

"Come on." He walked into the bank and witnessed Coco's signature, which was a scrawl unreadable to the average person. Coco could read and figure but his handwriting had never been his best achievement. The cashier handed over the money. Coco tucked it in his coat pocket.

They were wearing city clothes, dark coats, gray trousers, new Stetsons. They walked down to the hotel and Buchanan paid the bill. They went out back to the stable where Nightshade and Coco's big chestnut whinnied at them. Their gear was already stowed behind the saddles. They had been about to depart when Emory had interrupted them. They mounted and rode toward the railway station.

Coco asked, "What you think of that fat fella?"

"He talks too big."

"The money is good, though."

"Uh-huh, at least one thousand. But ten thousand . . . that's more'n you ever thought of gettin', win or lose."

"That's been rattlin' in my head."

"On t'other hand, you got one thousand. Can't take that away. So we ride down to Denver and see what else happens."

"On the train," said Coco. "I purely likes a train ride."

"I recall when there was no train to Denver. Town went down but the people hung together. Got the money and built the spur to the Union Pacific into Cheyenne." There had been a woman in those days, too. He could not shake the blond British lady from the forefront of his mind. Caroline Lamb. It was an odd but strangely familiar name. It had to do with reading. Off and on in lonely periods he had pored over a lot of books.

He shook himself. It was the time to think about Coco and the proposed fight in Denver. He knew the city was booming; it was the marketplace of the Rocky Mountains. It would be much more exciting than the last time he was there. Emory seemed to be on the level, at least he had come up with a thousand dollars. Where the next nineteen thousand was coming from was another matter.

There was no question that Coco would benefit by a win over Dan Ford. Paddy Ryan had been around a long time, and there was talk about a strong boy from Boston named Sullivan; none would fight a black man. If the newspapers carried the message that Coco was indeed a great fighter, the situation might, just possibly, be altered.

He had never tried to analyze his feeling for Coco. Since their meeting in El Paso some years back they had been as close as brothers. The simple honesty of Coco had appealed to the core of Buchanan. Hunt-

15

ing, fishing, riding, fighting together had been the finest times in the life of the big frontiersman. Coco's hatred and fear of firearms had come to make sense. There had to be an end to the senseless saloon killings, the offhand murders due to the handgun. The time had not yet arrived. Men like the Cutler cousins raided and thieved, the courts were not yet organized well enough, lawmen were mostly on their own, sometimes without proper local support. But Coco was basically correct. Civilization as such had to come to the West.

Buchanan was secretly glad in some ways that it had not yet taken hold. His experience with bankers, merchants, lawyers, townspeople had been seared with disillusionment. He vastly preferred the riders, the mountain men, many Indians of his acquaintance and a few of the women who were of the country. His respect for womankind went deep, he believed in them.

Lady Caroline was certainly not of the West, yet there had been something about her during the fracas in the Cheyenne Cattlemen's Club which attracted him in a most curious way. He would have to be very careful, he thought. Titled people from England just had to be a different breed.

A tall man wearing a badge stepped into the street and held up a hand. "Buchanan."

He reined in the big black horse. "Howdy, Marshal."

"You remember me?"

"Johnson. Back in Dodge City. You want somethin'?"

"Bit of a ruckus there, wasn't it?"

"Somewhat."

"Jepson, he's mighty mouthy. Carries weight, though. He wanted you arrested."

"Wanted? Or wants?"

"Had a talk with him. Everybody up and down the West knows you're a peaceable man. Never knew you to start up a fuss. Then a fella told me Jepson

16

was cussin' the ladies from England. Happen to know the gov'nor is high on those folks."

"Then we go about our business?"

"Just wanted to warn you. Jepson's rich and he's mean. If you run into him again, watch your back."

"I'll do that."

Johnson nodded toward Coco. "Your boy, there, he's goin' to fight a white man in Denver?"

"That's no boy. That's Coco Bean."

At the sharpness of Buchanan's tone, the marshal frowned, then managed a smile. "How do, Coco."

"How do, white man."

Buchanan said, "He's a champion, Johnson."

"There's some broken noses in town'll agree to that. You goin' down to the yard?"

"We're traveling with Emory and the British people to Denver," Buchanan said deliberately. "In the parlor car. You want to know anything more?"

"No . . . no," said Johnson. "Not bein' nosy. Nohow. Good luck to you. Both of you."

He stepped back and they rode on. Coco was grinning. Buchanan was inwardly fuming. Any slight to Coco because of his color made him highly irritable.

Coco said softly, "Don't you fret. The way it is, the way it always will be. I don't fret."

They came to the railroad yard. There was a man waiting. He showed them a freight car on a side track and asked, "You think you can get those nags up into it if I get me a ramp?"

Buchanan said, "I think you better get out of the way."

He rode Nightshade to the wide-open doors of the car and spoke softly in his ear. He dismounted and climbed into the car. The big black drifted a few feet, then seemed to take wings. He landed inside the car and slid to where Buchanan waited.

Coco's horse had been with them on the long trek. It hesitated, then, not quite so gracefully, followed

Nightshade. The railroad man gasped, then grinned. He was missing a tooth but his attitude was one of amazed admiration. He climbed into the car, a squat man with a revolver clumsily attached to a sagging belt and a whittled oaken club in one fist.

"If I heard, I wouldn't of believed," he said.

"My pa always said don't believe anything you hear and only half what you see," said Buchanan. "I do see you got hay and straw and a couple decent stalls. And a bag of oats, by golly."

"Knowed about hosses all my life," said the man. "Name of Jensen. You travelin' with them furriners?"

"Uh-huh."

"Got their own car. Never did see anything like that. But I gotta believe it. Had it special made in Chicago, they do say. Dukes and duchesses and all. Don't seem like they loco or nothin'. Pleasant folks. That's Coco Bean, ain't it?"

"Uh-huh." They were unsaddling the horses, wiping them down, dissatisfied with the ministrations of the livery stable. "We take great store by these animals. Make sure they get hooked up to the train, please."

"The crew'll handle that. 'Bout all I can do for you is show you the car with the dukes and all. Goin' to fight in Denver, Coco Bean?"

"Looks that way."

"I'll be a bettin' on you. Allus do." He waved as they gathered their bedrolls and leaped down to direct them.

Buchanan said, "That's not a good way to wear a gun, Jensen."

He showed his gap-toothed grin. "Never did use it. Just this when needed." He waved the staunch club. "Not much trouble around the yard, mostly young uns and hoboes."

"Uh-huh." Buchanan slipped him a silver dollar. "Bet it on Coco."

"Will do that." With a flourish he indicated the parlor car. "There 'tis. And the best of luck to you gents."

Brister was waiting to take their bedrolls as they climbed into the elongated car. Caroline Lamb was the first person they encountered in the narrow confines between baize-covered bunks. She smiled at Buchanan and led them to the small but elaborate sitting room in which the others awaited them.

There were firmly fixed candelabras giving light in the gathering dusk. There were velvet drapes at the windows, plush, deep carpet on the floor. A banquette lay along one side, the scenic side of the car. There was a long, narrow table laden with fruit, food from the Chinese restaurant kept hot by some alchemy, bottles and bottles of wine, beer and whisky, fine glass from which to sip, gleaming white napery, silver service traced with filigree engraving. It was a setting fit for a king—or a queen.

The Duke and Duchess of Comberland were ensconced in especially designed upholstered chairs fastened to the floor of the car for greater ease. They had wine glasses in their hands, their cheeks were flushed, they were smiling. Buchanan and Coco were waved to seats on the banquette. Lady Caroline and Brister presided over the feast of wine and delicacies.

The duke said, "Emory, of course, will go in the common carrier. Not one of us, what?"

"Not one of you? Or Coco and me?" asked Buchanan.

"Why, none of us." The duke seemed surprised. "A common fellow, isn't he now?"

Lady Caroline interposed. "Bertie means no harm. He is probably correct, you know. You are gentlemen of the great West we have so enjoyed. He is a . . . tradesman? Do you have tradesmen?"

"Some of my best friends are tradesmen," said

Buchanan. He waved away a proferred wine bottle. "Whiskey, if you please. Coco does not drink."

"Water with ice for Coco," said the duke. "Remarkable incident there at the—er—club, was it not? So swift. You two, splendid chaps. I really must see Coco fight."

"It will take some time. Denver's a mile high. He'll have to get used to the altitude."

"We have not been in Colorado," said the duke. "I have a hobby, y'know. I take pictures. Camera. Wet plates. How wonderful it's been, the bowl of blue sky in Wyoming and Montana, the Rocky Mountains. The deer, the coyotes, and a bear, a black bear, not yet a grizzly. Must get a grizzly."

"And the people," the duchess said suddenly. "The faces of the men, so strong. The women, plain but handsome."

"Now, that's interesting," said Buchanan. "How much did you shoot?"

"Oh, very little. Enough for food," said Lady Caroline. "Bertie isn't a killer."

"There've been others. Russians, Germans, some British," Buchanan told them. "They shot a heap of critters. Didn't eat 'em. Mostly took horns, hides."

"We have heard."

Buchanan said, "Lots of English ranch owners, comin' into the West. Big money people. Some real good folks."

"And fortunate they are," said the duke. "Alas, I have duties that require me to remain in my country."

"The country he loves," said his wife.

He regarded her with fondness. "Indeed. Dear old Britain." He raised his glass. "To the Queen, may she reign forever."

They all drank. It seemed proper to drain the glass. Buchanan's was immediately refilled by Brister.

He asked, "Mind if I ask how come you got mixed in with Charlie Emory?"

"Why, he was waiting for us in Cheyenne. Had a letter from a cousin in Britain. Knew I was in for sports and all. He showed us around the city. All that."

"Uh-huh." There was something tenuous about it. He began to see these people as innocents in a strange world, a world they had found beautiful, exciting, pleasurable; they had not the faintest notion of its complications.

Caroline said, "Bertie purely adores two things: the camera and the prize ring. He's taken his pictures, now he wants to see an American prize fight."

Bertie said, "We had a black champion, Molyneaux. Did you know of him?"

Coco said, "I know."

Buchanan added, "To your credit his race was not held against him."

"Ah, well," said Lady Caroline, "the Queen never acknowledged him. There are . . . problems. I am proud to say we do not agree."

Buchanan and Coco exchanged smiles. Talk drifted to other matters, the difference between the "tight little isle" and the wide-open spaces of the West, the bewildering conglomeration which was New York, the width and length of the Mississippi, the vastness of the plains, the destruction of the buffalo which had roamed by the millions, the distressful lot of the Indian. It was bright, intelligent talk and Buchanan enjoyed it. Mellowed by the fine, smooth liquor, encouraged by host and hostesses, he told stories of the early days on the trail, of Indian raids and conflicts with outlaws of every degree. Coco told of a fight in San Francisco Bay, of the one in Mexico which had nearly resulted in disaster. They told of their first meeting in custody of the Texas Rangers in El Paso.

The British people hung on every word. The ladies seemed able to keep up with the duke, drink for drink, without showing undue effects, until the available bottles were empty.

"Brister," called the duke. "Where are you, Brister? More wine, please."

As if in prompt response a man shouldered his way into the compartment. He was a big man dressed entirely in black from head to toe. He wore a black mask. Behind him crowded two who were only slightly smaller than he. They were all wide of shoulder, narrow of waist, graceful in bearing. Each carried a revolver.

Buchanan said, "Don't anybody make any foolish moves."

"A man after my own heart." The leader spoke softly, with a slight intonation of the Deep South in his voice. "And, Brother Buchanan, we know all about that little hidey gun in your belt buckle. Kindly put your hands behind your head."

Buchanan did as he was told. He was seething within at his helplessness, at his carelessness in not keeping watch. "The Cutler cousins, I believe."

"Names mean nothing," said the leader. "I don't wish to discomfort you good people. If you will just hand over your valuables. The necklaces from the ladies. Your purses, gentlemen. Place them upon the table."

Buchanan said, "You've heard about the 'drop,' folks. They got the drop on us."

"If you hurt Brister . . ." began the duke heatedly.

"A bit of a knock on the head. He'll be good as new in an hour," the leader said reassuringly. He was collecting the jewelry and the money while the other two held their guns ominously trained, very steady. Buchanan kept his eyes upon the ladies, upon the duke. He was afraid they would resist; he knew the consequences. Tales of the Cutler cousins abounded.

22

"We're not out to hurt folks," said the leader. This must be Cal Cutler, Buchanan thought. "Down where we come from the Yankees were not so considerate. Burned down our plantation, sent our black people off to wander homeless, were wicked to our women, stole our silver." He motioned to the silver on the table and one of the other men swept it into a gunny sack. "Jesse and Frank and the Youngers showed us the way, youall know. What they're doin' we aim to meet. And top." He laughed pleasantly.

Caroline was trying to remove a diamond ring. He waited, watching her. "Plenty of time, my dear lady. You are very beautiful, you know." He bowed at the duchess. "The emerald you are trying to hide. Not a good idea. We have use for gems. There are people who buy, no questions asked. It's a lot like London. Don't look much like it but people are critters wherever you go."

He took the emerald pendant. He turned to Coco. "Now, the thousand dollars. Give it to me, boy."

"What thousand dollars?" Coco asked.

"You know damn well what thousand dollars." For the first time the voice was harsh, dangerous. "Don't talk back to me, boy. Just hand it over and you'll live to fight again. Though I'll be bettin' the white man beats you."

Coco took out the money given him by Emory. Cal Cutler snatched it from him. He turned to the others, good nature resumed. "I know there's an iron safe here somewhere. I could blow it up. We could blow up the car with youall in it. You see? There would be no witnesses, we would be gone like ghosts in the night. We're not about to do such a thing. Just youall stay quiet until we get on our horses. Then you can wail to the moon. It's been a real pleasure."

They backed out. Buchanan glanced through the one unshattered window. He saw two men holding five horses. Each had a rifle at the ready. If he went for the little gun he would not only risk his own life, he would endanger them all. In complete frustration he watched the five masked men go into the night.

Then he saw movement to the right. He called out, "No! No, Jensen."

The yardman could not hear him. He was close enough to the robbers to claw out his revolver. He had it raised when the first shot rang out. Now Buchanan did slip the deringer from the ornate belt buckle. He plunged for the narrow entry to the door of the car.

He stumbled over the prone body of Brister, who was unconscious, his scalp bleeding. When he was able to regain balance and get to the vestibule of the car the riders were already running, melting shadows beneath a gibbous moon. He leaped to the ground. Coco came behind him with a lantern seized in the car. The British group appeared, the duke bearing a light hunting rifle.

Buchanan bent by the flickering light. Jensen stared up at him, a quizzical grin displaying his lack of an incisor. Buchanan said, "Just don't move. We'll get a doctor."

Jensen said, "Never had no trouble. It was the Cutlers, wasn't it?"

"Yes, the Cutlers."

"Bad people. Never knew they were hereabouts. Heard they were over . . . in . . . Montana. . . ." Jensen coughed. Blood ran from the corners of his mouth. "Bad, I got it. Never . . . thought . . . it would be . . . like this."

He died. Buchanan, a hand on the man's chest, felt the life go out of him. He knelt, silent, thinking of the simplicity of the yard man, his friendliness. There was no harm in this man. He was doing a job, not very well paid. He probably had a wife and family in the town. The revolver had been a joke, a mere tool. The odds were that if he had fired it he would not have hit anything. Yet he had tried. He had been ready to fulfill the duty assigned to him.

Lady Caroline Lamb knelt beside Buchanan. "Is he . . . gone?"

"Uh-huh."

"They shot him down like a dog? That well-spoken man?"

"Talk's cheap, Lady Caroline. They tell tales about the charity of the James Boys."

"The James Boys?"

"Murderers, believe me. Thieves and killers." He could not come to terms with himself. His revolvers were wrapped in his bedroll. His rifle was with his saddlebag. He, who had been through so many scenes like this, was helpless, unable to act. By the time he could saddle Nightshade and ride into unfamiliar country he would be a subject for ambush, his life would be sacrificed for nothing.

There were people coming with lanterns. He said, "Best you folks go back into the car. See about Brister. Leave this to me."

He was not proud of the story he had to tell. Marshal Johnson listened with a lip slightly curled.

Buchanan finished, "There was no outside look-see exceptin' poor Jensen. I should've figured that. Everybody thought the Cutlers were in Montana. I should've known they'd be wherever the loot is."

Johnson said, "Oh, you can't be blamed, Buchanan. They got you cold turkey just like they got everybody else. There's some, and mebbe I agree, that think they're tougher and smarter than the James Boys."

Buchanan looked hard at him. "No use to cry over spilt milk. No use me chasin' 'em in your country. But seems to me you should be raisin' a posse. It'll look better when the governor and the Washington bigwigs start askin' questions."

"Er . . . reckon you're right, at that." The marshal hustled off. Men carried Jensen to the wagon of the undertaker. Buchanan looked after them. He would not sleep well tonight.

2.

All the Cutler cousins were handsome. Divested of the black costumes, dressed as cowboys they were blond, curly-haired, with regular, open countenances. Cal, the leader, smiled at Chris and Con. They returned the smile, showing white, even teeth. The campfire was low, flickering shadows half-concealed the other two members of the band.

Cal said, "A nice haul. Not the biggest but very nice."

"The jewelry will bring in plenty," said Chris.

Cal touched the bandanna on which it lay, glittering. "If we don't keep it for the ladies."

Con said, "You keep yours for the women, Cal. I'm for buildin' the cash supply."

"You're back home before it is time," said Cal. "There's not near enough in the bank."

"The goddam Yankees," said Con, his face darkening.

"Bastard carpetbaggers," said Chris. "I aim to kill me a few of 'em."

"In due time," Cal told them. He called, "Toby, the whiskey."

Toby came bearing a bottle. Behind him came Stonewall, grinning. They were black men. They bore tin cups, five of them.

Cal poured with ceremony. They all raised the drinks. "To the Confederacy."

"Forever," chimed in the cousins.

"And damnation to all Yankees."

"Amen."

Cal put down his cup. He took a bundle of cash from a pocket. He counted out fifty dollars, divided it in two, handed each black man his half. "Better than playin' freemen, wandering, wondering, starving, eh, boys?"

"Yassuh!" They fondled the money, stowed it away. "We be free when you say so, boss man."

"You saw the nigger fighter?"

"We saw him," said Toby.

"Mixin' in with white folks. You know that's wrong."

"It ain't right, suh," said Stonewall. He was a brawny young man with close-cropped woolly hair.

Toby, slight but wiry, added, "You done taught us the right way, massuh. We knows what's best for us."

"What is best for all," said Cal. He picked up his cup and poured again, emptying the bottle. "We drink together but we know our places. Right?"

"Plain right."

Chris said, "If it wasn't for the fight comin' up, I'd have knocked that Coco Bean in the head."

"No," said Cal. "That is not our way. The yardman had to be killed. But always remember what I say: No violence unless it's absolutely necessary. Remember the James Boys. They killed that cashier and lost friends."

"They got enough friends to hide 'em out."

"Not the right kind of friends," Chris told them. "If you listen to me we'll return to Alabama and be rich. Powerful. Go into politics. Fight the damyankees on their own grounds."

They were silent. The dream was strong in them because Chris had implanted it. They had been boys in school during the war. They had borne arms, escaped death or imprisonment because of Chris. He was a natural-born leader and they were never without the belief that he could restore them to glory in the homeland."

Cal said, "All right, boys, stand your watches. That dumb Johnson'll never find us, but best to be careful."

The black men drew back from the low glow of the fire. The Cutlers stretched out on their blankets. They sipped their drinks.

Chris said, "Good thing you knew about Buchanan."

"Everybody in the West knows that son. A Texan, but he never fought for us. We sure put him down, didn't we?"

"Down under," said Chris.

"He's a big one," said Con. "Wonder if he can fight with his fists?"

"It's been said." Chris smiled.

"I'd like to bet you can whup him," said Con.

"I'd sure like to try him," said Cal.

"You were the champion."

"You boys were right behind me. Old Jake, he taught us good, didn't he?"

"Old Jake was the best nigger fighter ever lived. Too bad he was a slave."

"Pa made money off him fightin' other slaves," said Cal. "Money the Yankees got. Dug it up with the silver, the murderin' bastards."

29

"We'll get it back," said Chris. "And more."

He lay back with his head on the saddle. The pale moon was covered by a wisp of cloud. He said, "That blond lady, that would be somethin' to take back home."

"She sure would look good on the plantation," said Chris.

"Youall are woman crazy," grumbled Con. "I'm thinkin' of Holladay Street down in Denver. The whores are good enough for me 'til we get back home."

"She's one of those titled ladies," said Cal. "British. Bring new blood into the family."

"The family don't need new blood. Ours is good enough. Once we get back on top we can have any gal we want."

"Give me the home-grown," said Con. "Southern ladies know their place."

Cal closed his eyes. He could picture Buchanan helpless under their guns. He could see the face of the blond woman. He could relish the latest in their series of successes. He could sleep with the dream they shared.

Buchanan spoke softly to Nightshade. The black horse whinnied as if in sympathy. The revolvers were wrapped in oiled rags. Buchanan took them from the saddlebag and said, "Would have got me killed if I was wearin' them. Still and all." He replaced one and strapped the belt around his waist, feeling the comfort of the worn butt of the Colt with his hand. He closed the door of the car and walked back beneath the pallid moon.

A slim wrapped figure approached him. Lady Caroline said, "I can't sleep, thinking of that poor man."

"Uh-huh," said Buchanan. "I know how you feel."

"Trying to protect us . . . He was most helpful in

getting our luggage aboard. I—I've never seen a man dead . . . like that."

"I'm sorry to say, miss, that it happens in this country."

"It happens in my country also. It's just that I've been sheltered. We do not walk the streets of London alone."

"I should have been ready." His voice was bitter. "The Cutler cousins—it was thought they were in Montana. They move fast, those men."

"They are known, then. Will the marshal not catch them?"

"The marshal couldn't catch fish in a barrel."

"Then they'll go free to rob and kill again."

"Nobody ever caught the James brothers. And that's somewhat east of here. People, some people, make heroes of these gangs. They've been known to throw a bone to the poor."

"Robin Hood?"

"Not many know that story. But it's the same notion, I reckon. The poor are always against the rich. Bad men take advantage. It's real simple, miss."

"There was nothing simple about Jensen dying while we watched."

"No man's death seems simple to me," said Buchanan.

She put a hand on his arm. "I know you are deeply distressed."

"It would have been worse if anyone had made a move." He shook his mind free. "They knew too much."

"I'm afraid I don't know what you mean."

"They knew when to hit, while we were relaxed. They hit Brister too easy, too quick."

"Brister has been in our family for twenty years!"

"No, no. I mean, they knew the right time and place."

"But how could they? Who could have given them information?"

"They're smart. They've been smart right along, people say. But how did they know Coco had a thousand dollars on him? They're Southerners. People from down South don't expect a black man to be carrying that much money."

"From down South?"

"Negroes are considered no better than animals by educated Southerners. You could tell Cutler has been to school by his lingo."

"Lingo?"

"Scuse me. The way he talks. Good English but real slow-like."

She was puzzled. "But you talk slow and easy also."

"I guess you got to be a native, miss."

She said, "I expect so. And . . . I feel odd that you should call me 'miss.' "

"Your ladyship?"

"Caroline will do," she said. She smiled faintly. "I feel better after talking with you. I can still see that poor chap lying in his blood. I can still feel sorrow. However, you have a calming influence. Now—about the foreknowledge of the cutthroats who robbed us . . ."

"You been in town how long?"

"Just two days. Mr. Emory arranged everything for us so that we saw the city and the country close by."

"Mr. Emory—he's got good credentials?"

"Oh, yes. The best, Bertie says."

Buchanan shook his head. They turned back, walking in the long shadow of the car. "It'll be just another Cutler holdup, seems like. We'll be going to Denver tomorrow. Nobody knows where the Cutlers will be. I'm sorry about your jewelry and the money."

"Small loss compared to the death of a man."

"Uh-huh. The death of any man, it makes us all seem small."

They had come to the steps leading into the car. She hesitated. He picked her up by her narrow waist and set her on the vestibule floor. She gasped, then smiled, looking down at him.

"Thank you, sir."

"You're right welcome, miss . . . uh, Caroline."

The bobbing light of a lantern distracted him. He instinctively flattened himself against the car, warning her to go inside with a wave of his left hand. A man came running.

Buchanan said, "Stop right there, stranger."

The man said, "Uh, your highness, dukeship, whatever, there's been trouble down the tracks. We got to hook you up. I mean your car. We got to take it out tonight. Yard won't hold all the traffic."

Buchanan said, "Whatever you say." He climbed aboard and drew up the steps.

Lady Caroline said, "Which do you choose? Your dukeship sounds best to me."

"If you like it," he told her. He removed his sombrero as they slid into the car. There were sounds of snoring, of heavy breathing. The party slept.

She whispered, "A nightcap?"

"Never wear one," he told her, reaching for the sherry bottle.

"Fool!" she said. Her mood had switched; she was warm, friendly without reserve. "It was a bad moment or two back there. We mustn't let it affect us, must we? I mean, life and death, they come to us all."

"Jensen was doing what he was paid for. Still, they needn't have downed him." He poured for her.

She drank the sherry. He stuck to the whiskey. They sat in silence for several minutes. They found themselves exchanging self-conscious glances.

She said, "You know, I've never met a man like you, Buchanan."

"And I've never met a lady like you."

"Buchanan. That is Scottish."

"I reckon." The liquor was smoother than what he was used to. He poured another and she accepted a sherry. "My dad was born in East Texas. Never knew him good, he was a sheriff, got himself killed. Ma didn't last long after that."

"You were how old?"

"Fourteen."

"Fourteen and alone?"

"And busted. Broke. Without money. So I came west and went up the trail."

"Tell me about it."

The liquor had loosened his tongue. She listened with rapt attention, now and then asking a question. They spoke in low voices, not to disturb the others, and the bottles became empty. It was then they realized the lateness of the hour and arose, facing each other in the narrow space.

The car lurched. The coupling to the outgoing train was being made. The motion threw them into each others' arms. Again he felt the soft firmness of her slender body. There was a second uneven motion of the car.

She did not draw away, rather she clung to him to maintain balance. Their faces were close together.

She smiled, offering her lips. He kissed her, and her arms came up and tightened on his shoulders.

Coco said from deep sleep, "What's happenin' here?"

They sprang apart. Now everyone was up and rubbing eyes and wondering.

The duke said, "Ah, there. I take it we are on our way. Brister, are you quite all right?"

Brister, wearing a bandage on his head, was imperturbable. "More whiskey, sir?"

"More everything," said the duke. "Who can sleep

with all this goin' on? I say, Buchanan, are you and Carrie makin' a night of it?"

"Afraid we were gabbin' away," said Buchanan.

"I'm learning about the West. Nothing I have heard before matches what he has told me," said Lady Caroline. "I've been completely fascinated."

"It is the first time she has listened to a word anyone has said," the duchess observed. "A talker, is our girl, not one to sit quietly by, y'know."

"Yes, ma'am," said Buchanan. "I noticed."

She flushed but she did not cast down her eyes nor act bashful as would a country girl. She met his grin with one to match. Brister poured the drinks.

3.

The brand-new Windsor Hotel stood at the corner of Larimer and 18th streets. It was five stories high and sported a tower from which flew the American flag. From two lesser towers British flags waved in the wind. The sky was glorious, the view of the mountain splendid. Buchanan and Coco met Charlie Emory beneath a porte-cochere. Sparkling carriages drawn by matched teams moved in a stately way up and down. Larimer was the main street of the city.

"Over thirty thousand people," Emory bragged. "The hotel was built by an English company but Tabor owns it now. Tabor's worth millions, y'know."

"I heard of the man," said Buchanan.

"Them stables where we left the horses—we slept in worse places," said Coco. "Woo-ee, this-here is somethin'."

"They brought all Chicago hotel people out here to run the place," said Emory. "There's Billy Bush, now. Hi, there, Billy."

An overdressed man was seeing to the luggage of the duke's party, which was being delivered by a bewildered expressman. He waved but did not speak.

Emory said, "Should we go in and have a drink? Wait'll you see the bar. Got a funny Dutchman named Tammen working. Makes cocktails, mixed this and that. Real Chicago style."

"Never cared much for Chicago. The stockyards stink," said Buchanan. "Before we go in, let's talk about the robbery."

"Terrible thing. Mortifying," said Emory. "The duke has been real good about it. Still and all."

"Tell me, has anybody ever identified the Cutler cousins during a holdup?" asked Buchanan.

"Not that I know of. They always wear the masks . . . well, you saw them."

"Covered them complete." Buchanan nodded. "Can't tell if they're white or black, can't tell the color of their hair. Can't tell anything exceptin' they're Southern."

"Southern?"

"Deep south. The voice of the leader."

Emory said, "There's been stories. Some say they are niggers. . . . Scuse me, Coco, Negroes."

"What I'm gettin' at," Buchanan said, "is that they knew just when to hit us. And most important, they knew Coco had a thousand dollars on him. How do you account for that?"

Emory started, turned pale. "Hey, Buchanan! You're not hintin' . . . you're not sayin' . . ."

"I ain't the hintin' kind," Buchanan told him. "What I mean, there was a bunch in the Cattlemen's Club when you talked about the fight, showed the bank draft. Anybody could've heard us talkin'."

"That's right. They could have!"

"So. How many of them men did you personally know?"

Emory rubbed his chin. "Not all of 'em, that's for

sure. Jepson and Highpockets—that's his foreman, the one Coco laid out. A couple of the others. Cheyenne's not my town. Denver is where I hang my hat."

"Then one of the Cutlers or maybe one of their informers could have been in the club?"

"Informers? You mean like the James Boys, they've got people workin' for them?"

"The way I see it, they couldn't know so much and get around so easy if they didn't. And there's plenty people won't admit the war's over. Southern sympathizers, they're all over the West, come here when things went down in Dixie."

Emory said, "I tell you, gents, I don't know much about things of that kind. I'm out to make a dollar, like every other damn soul in this burg. Mind my own business when it comes to that sorta thing. I got good connections back east. The company that built this hotel, they know me. That's how I got to meet the duke and duchess."

Buchanan said, "Emory, that's none of my business. All I'm thinkin' on is the Cutler cousins. Let's mosey on inside this oversized mausoleum."

Emory started to speak, but checked himself. Coco and Buchanan shouldered their bedrolls. Buchanan's rifle was slung, his revolvers were now with him. He would not wear arms in the city but he could not, at this time, be far from them at any hour of the day.

The lobby was immense. Diamond-dusted mirrors abounded. The furnishings were lush, the strollers and loungers elegant in the latest styles. People stared at Buchanan and Coco, then looked away. There was enough of the frontier still abiding in them to accept whoever walked the tiled floor.

The desk clerk was polite. "Yes, gentlemen, the duke has spoken of you. You want a room together. It is arranged."

He tapped a silver bell and a uniformed, husky boy appeared and reached for the bedrolls. Buchanan waved him away, then followed as the desk clerk handed the boy a key. They went up in an elevator, no new experience to them. Their room was on the top floor.

Coco said, "I purely don't believe this. A fireplace?"

"One in every room," said the bellhop. "They really built this joint, didn't they?"

"I lived whole winters in cabins half this big," Buchanan said, staring around the huge room. He handed the boy a dollar. "I suppose we can order anything we want. If we pay for it."

"Mr. Emory says to put it on his bill. Whatever."

"Emory lives here?"

"Lots of people live here. Denver's full of people rich from the mines in Leadville, from this and that. I'm investin' in the Frisco market my own self."

"Shades be," said Coco. "No wonder they can pay off big for a prizefight."

"They can pay. And I'm bettin' on you. Dan Ford, he's not stayin' at the Windsor."

The boy departed. Buchanan went to a window and said, "If they got nothin' else, they sure got a view."

"It ain't no place to train," said Coco regretfully.

"Soon as the papers are signed we get out," Buchanan promised. "Best get the train dirt off and go down and see what's goin' on."

"One look at the town?"

"One look."

"Just you and me?"

"If we can lose the duke." But he was thinking of Lady Caroline and the brief kiss and how she had smiled at him. He wondered why she affected him more deeply than any woman he could remember. It was certainly not because she was titled and British.

He was indifferent to such matters. There was something—exciting—about her. It lay within her, not on the surface. He told himself that time would tell, as it always did. Still, he was dissatisfied.

Coco was looking at his striped gray and white suit. It was wrinkled from traveling in the bedroll, as was all the clothing they carried. Buchanan pulled the bell cord, as the bellboy had suggested.

A fresh-faced red-haired girl appeared. She curtsied and in a brogue that could be cut with a dull knife said, "Is it somethin' I could do, now?"

"We need a pretty girl with an iron."

"Maureen O'Dea, sir. And what would you have done?"

He showed her the garments. She said, "Sure, it'll take awhile until me iron is hot."

Buchanan produced a silver dollar. The girl beamed and said, "But not too long thereafter."

Coco said, "We got to go downstairs in what we're wearin'."

"Clothes don't make the man."

"Clothes make him feel a lot better if they're nice."

Buchanan said, "Brush up. Shake 'em out. We're clean, that's what matters."

Thus they went down in the elevator in their traveling outfits, durable but not smart. There was a crowd of people in the lobby. Foremost among them was Charlie Emory, flushed and full of importance. He made a dramatic gesture and cried to them, "Just in time! Just in time!"

There was a knot of people around a towering man with a craggy nose and a bent ear. He had bright blue eyes and a merry twinkle. He was dressed in clothing too tight and brogans fit for a behemoth. Beside him was a tiny aged man with a fierce demeanor and a bowler hat which sat cockily to one side of a round head.

Emory cried, "Coco Bean, heavyweight champion of the West, this here is Dan Ford and his manager, Tony Burgess. And also let me announce the presence of Tom Buchanan, handler and friend to Coco Bean!"

Reporters from the *Rocky Mountain News* and the *Post* scribbled notes. Sporting figures crowded close and Emory had trouble keeping a space clear for the principals of his venture.

The voice of Bertie Lamb, Duke of Comberland, came strongly but politely above the hubbub. "May I please? If you gentlemen will just form a semicircle and face me?"

He had his camera on a tripod. He was flushed and earnest. When Emory pronounced his name with a flourish, he waved a hand and ducked beneath a black canopy behind his camera. "Smile, please. . . . Hold it!"

Buchanan found himself obeying. It was not the first time he had posed for a photograph. The men from New York were also experienced, he saw. Coco moved close to him and froze. The duke held his flash-pan high. It exploded and two of the sports reached inside their coats and produced sawed-off revolvers, spinning, looking for invasion.

"Once more, please," said the duke, nimbly changing plates.

They posed again. Buchanan felt the presence of the big fighter from the East, who stood beside him, a quiet, commanding figure. The man had sloping shoulders and long arms. His hands were not unnaturally large; the knuckles were bent in from the fighting. After the second flash he looked at Buchanan and smiled. Gold teeth shone.

"We've heard about you, Mister Buchanan. They tell tales, eh?"

"Lies, mostly," Buchanan told him. "But they don't lie about Coco. You'll have a good fight."

"Aye, man, that's why I'm here. It'll decide somethin', now, won't it?"

"It will."

The little man named Burgess skittered between them. "None of the guff, you Buchanan. Don't be tryin' any of your fancy on us. Dan'll beat your black man to blazes."

"Now, Tony," said the fighter in his rather high, rather soft voice. "This is a man of the West. Be polite, Tony."

Buchanan was scarcely paying attention. Brister was shouldering the tripod and toting the camera. The duchess was smiling at a reporter. Lady Caroline was carrying paraphernalia connected, he supposed, with the taking of pictures. She was smiling, tall, looking over heads. He waved to her and she nodded and shrugged, indicating that she could not at this moment speak with him. At least he hoped that was what she meant.

Emory cried, "All right. Everyone to the bar. Drinks are on me."

It was the magic call of the wild. They poured into the saloon. The bar was sixty feet long. There was a ballroom with exquisite crystal chandeliers and parquet floors. The mob flocked to the bar as Emory beckoned to Buchanan and Coco and Ford and Burgess. They followed him to a side room, with tables and chairs imported from England, waiters in attendance, floors thick with carpet of deep scarlet hue. When the door was closed there was a hush. They seated themselves. Emory produced folded papers.

He said, "The terms have been agreed upon, right, gentlemen?"

They nodded. The waiter brought pen and ink. Burgess put his nose to the contracts, his lips moving as he read. Buchanan scanned his copy, passed it to Coco. Papers meant little to either of them, they relied upon people as they saw them. Emory seemed to be all right—at least he had the backing.

Dan Ford said, "I heard about what happened to your advance, Coco. Lemme buy drinks."

"I'll take a glass of milk and thank you," said Coco.

Burgess looked up and snarled, "Don't be throwin' yer mazoola away on enemies, y' dumb fool."

"Now, Tony." Ford smiled at the others. "Tony likes to play mean. He's been good to me. If you could excuse him?"

"We take people as they come," Buchanan told him. "It's a pleasure to meet a man like yourself."

"I am a fighter. That doesn't make me a thug," said Ford. "I had a good father and a wonderful mother. They taught me not to talk big. Act big, fight big, but don't be big mean."

Coco said, "It's goin' to be hard to beat on you, Dan Ford. You the finest gentleman I ever agreed to fight."

"Will you please sign the papers?" Emory pled. "This is the biggest sportin' event ever happened to the West. Denver is behind it, the whole city. Trains'll be comin' in for it from all over the country. And from England, Ireland and Wales that I know about, thanks to the duke sending out word. I got to get some other fighters on the bill. I got a million things to do."

Burgess said, "Seems there ain't no tricks in it. Gimme the pen." He signed and Dan Ford signed.

Buchanan said, "You're excused, Charlie." He watched as Coco signed.

Emory asked, "What about you, Buchanan?"

He shook his head. "I'm in his corner. Coco is the boss."

"You let a nigger boss you?" snapped Burgess. "You ain't got guts enough to put your name onna line?"

44

Buchanan smiled at him. "I don't need guts. Coco has them."

"You tryin' to say my man's soft? Just because he talks nice like a damfool? You tryin' somethin' on us?" He was like a banty rooster, bridling.

Buchanan said, "If I was, you'd be an easy target, little man. Why don't we just cut this short and go down to Holladay Street and see what's happenin' in the sinks of iniquity?"

Burgess jerked back his head, looked down his nose. "You may be a big dummy, but you do have an idee, there. Where's those drinks?"

Emory put the contracts back in his pocket. "You boys have fun. Charge anything but gamblin' money to me."

He was gone. Buchanan watched the waiter bring a bottle of Monongahela whiskey and a bottle of cold milk. It must be Tabor money or city money, he thought. Emory could never afford all this largesse on his own. It made no difference, excepting an unlucky incident could leave Emory hanging on a limb—and that the contracts were made out in Emory's name. It was something he was not going to worry about, he decided. He noted that Dan Ford accepted whiskey. That was something to remember. They drank and Burgess fussed and Coco talked with Ford, and Buchanan relaxed, in the mood for exploration and some fun in the pits of Denver. He had not gambled in a long while, and in him there was always the small, impish urge to bet upon his judgment of cards, dice or a wheel.

He said, "Gents, excuse us. Coco and me, we got to change clothes." He finished his drink.

Coco said, "Wait for us, now. We need protection in this tough city."

Burgess snarled at them. Ford laughed in his easy way. They took the elevator to their room.

Maureen O'Dea was on hand. Their clothing looked

45

like new. Buchanan gave her another dollar. She lingered, dimpling, grinning at them.

"Goin' on the town, are ye? Mind yourselves, now. Holladay Street, all those flighty ladies and bad men."

"What's the best place to gamble a little?" asked Buchanan.

"What I hear—hear, mind ye—is that Mme. Velvet's the only honest dealer in the city. Hard men go there. Good men, bad men, no one touches Mme. Velvet. And I do hear she is an Irish lady. Her name, no one knows, her true name."

Buchanan said, "Mme. Velvet it is, then."

She laughed. "And good luck to you and bad cess to your enemies." She did her little curtsy and departed.

Buchanan said, "Now, there's a nice piece. Better than those we'll be seein', no doubt."

"You been in the tulies too long," said Coco. "You got women on your mind."

"You think?"

"I know. You and that Lady Car'line."

Buchanan said, "I reckon it's you been in the boonies too long. Got your head rollin'."

There was a knock on the door. The bellhop had a folded stiff piece of notepaper for Buchanan. He read, "The Duke and Duchess of Comberland would enjoy your company at dinner. How is that for pompous bulldrops? . . . Bertie."

He was tempted. He looked at Coco, all dressed in his best and ready to go. He said to the boy, "Please tell the duke and duchess I've got a previous engagement."

He gave the boy a coin. Coco rubbed his head.

"You turnin' down Lady Car'line? Is it because I said somethin'?"

Buchanan grabbed him by the ear and led him to

46

the door. "You're gettin' to have a real big mouth. Let's get down and join our friendly enemies."

But as he went to the elevator he realized that he would rather have met with the pleasant British people for the evening. When they came down to the lobby and saw Ford and the little manager waiting he also knew he could not have backed out of the projected excursion into the netherworld of Denver.

Burgess snarled, "Where you bums been? I'm hungry."

Buchanan looked down at him, amused. "You ever say anything that ain't an insult?"

"Not if I can help it."

They went into the huge, elaborate dining room. Waiters in severe black and white, on silent feet, appeared to lead them to a table. Their arrival had been foreseen, their dinners ordered, it seemed. Piping-hot soup, green in color, came from a gold-engraved tureen. Turtle soup, Buchanan recognized from his days in the fleshpots. Then there was fish and then roast beef carved at tableside, with potatoes au gratin, fresh tomatoes. . . . He lost track of the viands. He did, however, eat of each dish with great relish. Ford and Coco, already conscious of training for the fight, ate sparingly, but Burgess kept up with Buchanan, mouthfuly by mouthful. The little man was extraordinary; Buchanan wondered where he put it all.

When they had at last finished, a waiter presented a bill. It was for almost a hundred dollars but he asked only that Buchanan or Burgess sign it. The little man snatched it and wrote with a flourish.

"Now let's go get some women," he said. "I hear the city is bustin' with 'em. Let Emory pay."

They went down to Holladay Street, which the city fathers had thought to name after the great stagecoach entrepreneur, Ben Holloday, but had not learned how to spell his name. It was teeming with people, all kinds of people. Denver had become a hub of the West, as usual because of the railways. Its beginnings had been lurid. Evidently no one stood in the way of its continuing wildness.

Brothels of all descriptions, gambling halls and saloons lined Holladay Street. Barkers shouted the enticements of each palace of sin. Men walked, usually in pairs or in groups. Thieves and pickpockets were known to live high off the denizens of the area.

Buchanan paused before a stone building more imposing than the others. Over the door was a stone figure of a woman in a long skirt, a low neckline and high-piled hair. Beneath the figure were chiseled script letters. "Madame Velvet." There was a man standing in the doorway but he did not shout blandishments; he wore a tin star and a scowl.

Buchanan said, "This is the place they told us about."

"A copper," said Burgess. "I ain't much for coppers."

Buchanan ignored him, went to the door. Coco followed, as did Dan Ford. Burgess, cursing beneath his breath, tagged along. The doorman was polite, saying only, "No guns, mind you. This here is the quiet place."

They entered. It was indeed quiet. The ceiling was cathedral high; chandeliers to rival those of the Windsor Hotel gave glittering light. There were two winding stairways leading up to a series of oaken doors. As they watched a beautiful black girl and a foppish white man entered one of the rooms.

Coco muttered, "Nicest place in town? I'd like to see the worst."

"They ain't makin' a fuss," said Dan Ford. "Live and let live, says I."

There were the sounds of clicking wheels, bouncing dice and the slap of cards overset by murmuring voices. The dealers were all clad alike, in white shirts with sleeves rolled, gray striped trousers and polished black boots. Among them floated a small figure, now and then taking the case at faro or spinning a wheel or sitting in for a hand of poker.

She was small and dark, a young woman with an hourglass figure on a small scale. Her dress was clinging white, with gold embroidery, neither daring nor modest. A sentinel from a tall chair stepped down and touched her arm with deference, pointing to the four newcomers. She turned and Buchanan saw that she was indeed beautiful; sharply chiseled nose, large round dark eyes, smooth shoulders, perfect skin, gleaming, regular white teeth. She seemed to float as she approached them.

Her voice was low and husky, almost the voice of a boy. "Mr. Buchanan? And friends?"

"How do you do? This is Tony Burgess, Dan Ford and my close friend, Coco Bean."

"I have heard of you, all of you. So happy to have you in my establishment. What is your pleasure?"

Burgess said flatly, "I wanta look over the gals."

She looked only at Buchanan, face tilted back, a small smile in her eyes. "Use discretion, Mr. Burgess. My girls are all ladies."

Burgess was about to retort when she turned her remarkable eyes directly upon him. He swallowed and said, "Like you say."

Buchanan shook his head. "He has to be like that."

"Truth to tell," said Ford, "there's little harm in him."

"The games are honest," said Mme. Velvet. "You pay your money and take your chance."

"So we've heard," Buchanan told her. He watched Coco and Ford drift off. Coco was leading his future opponent to the squarest of all Western games, faro. Under Buchanan's tutelage Coco had become proficient at bucking the bank.

Mme. Velvet put a hand on Buchanan's forearm. "Would you like to look around?"

"I been in a lot of gamblin' palaces but this tops 'em all," he said. "I'd admire to make a pasear."

They strolled around the perimeter of the big hall. The players were a mixed bunch, prospectors fresh from a strike, ranchers in Stetsons and boots, the demimonde in city garments. Whiskey was carried to the players by short-skirted girls. It was decorous indeed.

She said, "You notice the policeman at the door? I'm the only proprietor who insists on protection for the money I pay in graft. My lookout men do not carry guns. It is well known that we never have trouble here."

"Never is a long time," Buchanan said. "All the money around here, it could bring in the greedy."

"We're all greedy," She laughed on a note to match her voice. "And what's your game, Mr. Buchanan?"

"Tonight? Poker."

"Stud?"

"The best."

"Right here, sir." She led him past a whirring wheel to a corner table. Two blond young men, a well-dressed citizen and a miner were accepting cards from an eye-shaded house man. Mme. Velvet waved and the house man departed. She took his place. Buchanan seated himself, watching her handle the deck with great skill and grace.

One of the blond man said, "Been waitin' on you, madame. Always a pleasure."

"Thank you, Sonny. Meet Mr. Buchanan. And Bo Reiner from Leadville and Dr. Hopper . . . Sonny Gilbert and Harry Jackson . . ."

"Howdy," said Buchanan. The others seemed to know one another.

"Five card stud, nothing wild, sky's the limit,"

said Mme. Velvet, all business. She dealt with the speed of a magician at work.

Buchanan took out a poke of gold pieces. The other players all had hard money before them. Mme. Velvet held the deck and said, "Ace bets, Mr. Buchanan."

Without looking at his hole card, watching the others, Buchanan said, "One hundred dollars."

"Call," said the miner.

"Call," said Sonny. "You're a well-known man, Mr. Buchanan. For poker among other things."

"Uh-huh," said Buchanan. He saw the other man hesitate, then throw in. Mme. Velvet looked at her hole card and put a hundred dollars in the pot. She began to deal, slower now for dramatic effect. "A ten and a jack and a deuce . . ."

Into the peaceful quiet of the establishment came the roar of a voice which brought everyone around in astonishment. "All right. Nobody move. We got you covered."

Buchanan slid back from the table. There were men on either side, high above. They held shotguns. There was a tall man at the door. The policeman was shoved in and fell to the floor as two men stood in the doorway behind their leader.

The man called Sonny said, "I be a raccoon's motha."

Mme. Velvet said, "God, they'll finish me for good."

Buchanan sought out Coco and Ford. They were standing at the faro table, motionless. Yet he saw they were poised, fighting men ready to explode. There was no sign of Burgess.

The invaders were all masked. The leader called out, "This here is the Cutler cousins and friends. You know what that means."

"Uh-huh," muttered Buchanan. "It means you're bullin' us."

The two men in the doorway produced gunny sacks. They walked to right and left of the room.

The leader called, "Just put all the cash in them sacks. Remember we're watchin' from every damn place. Cheat us and you're deader'n Adam."

Buchanan's eye caught movement behind a gunman on the balcony. A door opened, then swiftly closed. He thought he recognized the sharp features of Burgess. His mind went rapidly over the situation. Lookout men without guns were helpless. The policeman had been easily disposed of. Without weapons there was no chance of resistance. His right hand went to his belt. The masked man with the sack was approaching them. Mme. Velvet was swearing beneath her breath.

Again there was stealthy action on the balcony. The robbers were not brilliant, Buchanan thought. They had not taken into consideration the men who had chosen women for their amusement. This time it was the door through which the foppish dude had passed.

The robber came to the table and said, "Hiya, madame. Lemme ask you to stick all that money in this here." He thrust the sack beneath her nose.

On the balcony Burgess appeared. He had in his hands a large, heavy lamp. He raised it high, then crashed it down on the head of the robber. He yelled. "Danno! Get 'em!"

"The damfool," said the man called Sonny. At the same instant he drew a Bowie knife from behind his neck and stabbed the man with the gunny sack.

Buchanan slipped the deringer from his belt buckle into his right hand. He aimed with care. He shot the leader through the head.

The fop appeared. He sank a glistening blade into the back of the second gunman.

Now Ford and Coco went into action. Moving so swiftly that the confused, startled robbers could not bring their weapons into play, they swing hard fists.

One gun went off. A dealer went down even as he

fled. Blood stained the thick carpet. Buchanan shot the murderer with the second bullet in his deringer. In a moment the texture of the scene had completely changed, and Mme. Velvet was on her feet, crying for order.

One of the blond young men said to the other, "Sonny, we better take off."

"Yeah. Back door okay, madame?"

"Certainly." She leaned against Buchanan. "The police will be here any minute. Such a shame."

Sonny said, "I've heard about that little gun of yours, Buchanan. Proud to have been here when it was helpful."

"Dr. Hopper," said Mme. Velvet. "Could you look at my man? The blood . . . it's so awful."

Burgess was strutting, Ford and Coco behind him. "Fool around with guys from the Five Corners, will they? I seen worse'n them in N'Yawk more'n once."

"You might've got us all killed," Buchanan said sharply. "It was a damn fool play, Burgess."

"It worked, is all I care. I ain't givin' up money to thieves, like you an' Coco did. Them Cutlers ain't all that tough."

"That wasn't the Cutlers," said Buchanan.

"Said so, didn't he? Man knows who he is, don't he?"

"Like you just reminded us so helpful, I saw the Cutlers. I heard the boss man talk. Not the same people."

"Whoever. I don't give a hoot. We got 'em, didn't we?"

Police were now coming through the door. The cop who had been on duty was dead of a broken neck. The robbers remaining alive were roughly handled as they were taken into custody. None of them was blond, none particularly Southern in speech.

Mme. Velvet stayed very close to Buchanan. "I'm

53

so happy you're here. They all respect you. Please stand by me."

"Don't you worry, ma'am," Coco told her. "He's right there these days when a woman—uh—needs him."

Buchanan glared at him. Then he was talking with the police, giving them a graphic true account, discounting the widely repeated statement that the Cutler cousins had at last been run to ground. Mme. Velvet never let go of his arm. It was more and more pleasing to him. She was a truly beautiful woman.

The two blond young men walked in leisurely fashion up 18th Street, past the Windsor Hotel. The one who called himself "Sonny Gilbert" said, "Imagine havin' that son Buchanan around when he was needed like that."

"You see him produce that nasty li'l ol' gun?"

"Could I miss?"

"You come on good with the Bowie, Cal. But it wasn't a good play."

"You snuck the cash off the table real good, Con. Nobody else thought about the money."

"Yeah. Hey, imagine that bastid sayin' they was us."

Cal Cutler said, "Too bad Buchanan wouldn't believe it. Could've switched attention away from us for a long time."

"They say that's what happens with the James Boys. Every time a bank goes down back East they get the blame."

"You reckon we're goin' to be as famous as they are?"

"If we work hard," said his cousin.

They turned off on a peaceful side street and went into a boarding house run by a Southern lady named Rosalie Hightower. The third cousin was playing cards with three elderly women. He excused himself and the three went upstairs and foregathered in the room occupied by Cal.

The story was told. Cal ended, "And that Buchanan is just as quick and as mean as people keep sayin'."

"What about Madame?"

"Fine little lady. Maybe after we do our job we'll stop by there. Lots of money loose around there."

"But the other job first."

"Why, sure. It's the biggest. It'll beat anything Jesse and them ever pulled."

"Buchanan."

"We'll be watchin' for Buchanan."

"A big motha, ain't he? Think you could whup him, Cal?"

"Any man whups Buchanan will be considered the biggest in the West." He had thought about fighting Buchanan since he had first laid eyes on him. It was a dream to live by. "Could it be arranged, I'd be proud to meet him."

He doubled his fists. He had the size, he was younger, he had the will to win. Yes, he would be glad to make the fight, to be the biggest man in the West.

4.

Charlie Emory was distraught. He rubbed his bald head and cried in his weepy voice, "You gotta train here. I can sell tickets. This is where the people are, the big city."

Buchanan shook his head. "Cities. You saw what happened in Cheyenne. You know what happened at Mme. Velvet's."

"Boulder's to hell and gone up in the mountains. Nobody's goin' there to see Coco train."

"We'll make do."

"What about sparrin' partners?"

"I've sent telegrams to those we want."

Emory recognized defeat. "If you got to go, then you got to go. But it's money down the drain."

"Just make sure you get up the purse," Coco said. "I'm already out one thousand."

"The money is here, don't worry. Denver's right proud of this bout. Don't worry your head about money."

Buchanan said, "We'll let you do that. Let's go, Coco."

They rode the horses. The train would bring up the equipment. As they left town they took deep breaths of the fresh mountain air. Peace settled upon them. It was a slowly ascending road through glorious country, and they savored every mile of it.

A brace of antelope cantered across their path and Buchanan waved to them. In this setting he was exuberant. "The hills look like they're good for gold. The grazin's good for cattle. You know how old the town is?"

" 'Bout twenty-five years, they say. Air's mighty thin."

"Thinner than Denver. Cleaner, too." Snow was atop the Continental Divide, in the distance. "You'll get used to it."

"I better had. That Dan Ford, he ain't mean but he's a big un."

"And quick."

"And quick." Coco rode awhile in silence, then asked, "How we gonna get fixed here? How we gonna train and all?"

"The duke has a friend. Name of Reiner. Mine owner."

"The duke's got friends everywhere, seems like. 'Course his sister, she's already there." Coco chuckled. "Twixt her and Mme. Velvet you truly becomin' a lady's man."

"Shush your mouth."

Two railroads had come to Boulder in 1873, the Colorado Central and the Denver & Boulder Valley. The duke and his entourage had gone ahead with enthusiasm to set up training quarters under the offices of Bob Reiner. It seemed that the mine owner had been to England and had somehow fallen in with the affable, democratic nobleman. At mention

58

of Reiner's name Lady Caroline had blushed. Buchanan had not failed to notice.

Young people were everywhere as they rode in. The college had been established in 1861 and provided the city with life, color and capital from the pockets of the students.

Pearl Street stretched wide. The buildings were compact, made of stone and timber from the hills. It was, Buchanan saw, a small but busy city.

Coco said, "Looky yonder. They sure are expectin' somethin'."

There was a banner stretched from the bank building across to a pole. People were on the walks. A band began to play "Hangtown Races."

"I be doggone," said Buchanan.

The banner was lettered, "Welcome to Coco Bean, Champion." Now they could see the duke and duchess and Lady Caroline. The duke had his camera ready. Caroline was waving a kerchief. Cheers rang out, people called their names.

"Just like we amounted to somethin'," said Coco.

"Smile. Wave at 'em."

"Where we goin' to?"

"Hotel down the street." He pointed to a tall man staring at them. "All the way from Wyoming. What's his name?"

"Called the man Highpockets," said Coco. "Works for that Jepson fella."

"Uh-huh." It was something to think about. He bowed and waved, as he had seen dignitaries perform when on parade. Someone had certainly acted quickly to get a turnout like this. He was not sure whether or not he enjoyed it. Public attention did not exactly thrill him. A man was a target, riding the middle of the street through a crowd.

They dismounted at the hotel. A local reporter asked obvious questions and then the duke and his party were there, escorted by Bob Reiner, who showed white teeth and held fast to the arm of Lady Caroline. Out of the corner of his eye Buchanan saw the tall man from Wyoming duck into the telegraph office across the street.

The band was playing "Buffalo Gals." The people surged forward. Bob Reiner raised a hand and a covey of brawny giants formed a line blocking them off.

He said, "Please, friends, our heroes are weary from their ride. Allow them to rest. Remember, we shall all be seeing Coco training up at the camp."

The band wheeled around and marched away. The crowd followed. Reiner led the party inside the hotel and to the bar. It was a modest establishment but in apple-pie order. Buchanan became aware that Reiner was indeed a power in Boulder.

The duke's party sat at a long table. Lady Caroline came and pulled Buchanan to a chair and smiled at him.

Buchanan said, "Did I hear about camp? Is it set up?"

"We managed, the duke and I. He's already taken pictures of it." Reiner was pleased with himself.

"Cabins. A large tent or two," said the duke. "Good job. Reiner's been more than helpful."

"I'm obliged," Buchanan said.

"I have sparmates for you until the professionals arrive," said Reiner. "Those big fellows you saw. Strongest of the miners hereabouts. One of them has had some experience."

Coco said, "How much experience, I wonder? Tom, this is gettin' to be a circus, ain't it?"

"Might's well have stayed in Denver." Buchanan was not comfortable. He said to Caroline, "Excuse us, please? The long ride, we need cleanin' up a bit."

She said, "One drink."

He accepted. It was whiskey from the duke's locker.

It mellowed him for the moment. Bob Reiner came and smiled.

"I'll bet you want to wash up."

Buchanan said, "Readin' my mind. Thanks."

Reiner led them to a rest room off the bar. Buchanan closed the door.

"Reiner, you been fine. It's all real nice. But we're here to train for a fight and already I spotted a galoot that don't like us in the crowd."

"Why—we only mean to be friendly." Reiner was genuinely surprised.

"Man called Highpockets. Tall, skinny jasper. Works—or did work—for Jepson up in Wyoming."

"Jepson, the rancher?"

"That's him."

"I don't know of anyone representing Jepson down here."

"Uh-huh. Well, if you'll give us a guide and excuse us to the company we'll mosey on up to wherever."

"I reserved rooms for you. . . ."

"Decent of you." Buchanan stared at him.

Reiner said, "Whatever . . . I mean, the duke, Emory, they're good people. They have provided us with funds, information about your needs, all that. Do you want the sparmates to go along? Right now, that is?"

"Good idea," said Buchanan.

Reiner hesitated, then nodded. "I think I see what you mean. A lot at stake, you want to get to work. Like you say, Buchanan. See you outside in a few minutes."

Coco waited until Reiner was gone, then said, "You got the wind up, Tom."

"You got a hard fight comin'. We never heard from those pugs we telegraphed. Yeah, I got anxiety."

Outdoors they found the three miners. Their names were Alex, Tony and Dax. They were hard-bitten and they wore smiles, as if they knew something private. They rode mules. Reiner introduced them and went back to the party.

From the hotel steps Lady Caroline called, "See you tomorrow, gentlemen. Good hunting."

Buchanan waved. The miners rode out of town to a winding rocky road and began a climb. The road was steep and led to the edge of a stream which rippled and sang.

"Boulder Creek," said Alex, who seemed to be the leader of the trio. "Runs like a river, an't?"

"Like a real stream," Buchanan acknowledged.

"Overflows like a flood," said Alex. "Camp's a bit higher, not too close, an't?"

"Whatever yous say." The miner's accent was foreign, probably Welsh. Buchanan thought about the man called Highpockets, the strange fact that the sparmates he had called in had not appeared and various other matters. Events were not out of hand but the signs were not propitious.

The campsite was on a level spot in the mountains, seven thousand feet above sea level, and still the peaks loomed high about them. It was late afternoon and the sun struck black holes here and there, some of them working mines, others played out. They dotted the otherwise pristine glory of the scene.

Buchanan and Coco stared at the camp. There were cabins, there were tents. There was a large tent that contained the boxing ring. There was a cookhouse, and a black man came forward to greet them.

"Name of Crocker," he told them. He was short and round and his grin was expansive. "Didn't know you was a comin' but I got vittles for an army. Howdy, howdy."

Buchanan said, "We can eat."

"Never seen such a layout in my whole born days," Coco said. "Must be the duke, you reckon?"

"The duke. And Mr. Reiner," said Buchanan. "Too many people."

"Let's us eat and sleep," said Coco. "I'll be runnin' in the mornin'. It'll take a time for me to get used to this kinda thin air."

"Which is why we're here." The location was splendid, no question about it. Of course it was the biggest fight operation in which Coco had ever been involved. They were doing it up brown, all right. Still, he was uneasy. The glimpse of Highpockets, the stream of events, the violence which had gone before had left him with his sixth sense vibrating. He had a deep sensitivity for danger bred in his life on the frontier. It was working now, even as he surveyed the peaceful, beautiful scene.

Crocker knew how to cook, plain food, huge portions. They ate and went to the cabin and found two bunks which were comfortable. The sound of Boulder Creek lulled them to sleep.

Coco was awake at dawn. He ran up the road, higher and higher, and his breath became shorter and shorter. He saw squirrels and deer and a coyote slinking in the brush and he heard birds sing in the trees. And then he heard low explosions. He started, always fearful of and hating the sound of guns. Then he realized it was the miners at their work. He turned and came down the road to the camp. He felt lightheaded. It would take time to become accustomed to fast movement in this high country.

There were new arrivals in camp. Buchanan was talking with Lady Caroline. The duke was taking pictures with the duchess and Brister in attendance as usual. Coco slipped into the cook tent. Crocker greeted him and waved him to a small table. The odor of ham and eggs was strong on the air.

Crocker said, "I swan, this here is somethin' for me. On account of you I got me a small bank account in Boulder. Never thought to meet up with you."

"Glad to see one of us is makin' somethin'," said Coco.

"There's others. Us niggers got it pretty good here. Mr. Reiner, he's a good man. I works for him."

"That's fine."

"A man that thinks about us. Rich, too."

"He puts this camp together?"

"You bet. That English duke feller, he talked to Mr. Reiner and they sorta got together. Did it up brown, didn't they?"

"They did. But they'll be paid, one way or t'other."

"Mr. Reiner, he's a sport. He's bettin' a bunch on you."

"They do bet," said Coco. "Like everybody but me."

"You don't bet on you?"

"Tom and me, we seldom."

"You and him. There's stories goin' around. My, oh, my! A nigger with a white friend like Buchanan."

"Yeah. People do talk." It was a friendship as close as two men could enjoy. It had endured over the years. There had never been really bad times. Dangerous, yes. Close to death in many places under many conditions. But they had stuck, Tom and Coco, and thus far it had been for the best. He dug into the food with gusto. He would take a nap and then get into the ring with the miners. He worried some about them. To him they looked muscle-bound.

He knew he'd have to be in tiptop shape to beat Dan Ford. The big man was gentle and polite, somewhat like Buchanan. Men like that were devils when aroused. The absence of experienced sparmates could be disastrous. He wondered if someone had bought them off. Of course some were busy, could be a few had signed up for the preliminary fights and wanted no part of facing Coco before the event.

He sensed that Buchanan was worried and it affected him. He ate slowly, wrinkles across his broad brow.

* * *

Lady Caroline was wearing Western garb, a divided skirt, soft leather boots, a man's shirt. They became her very well. Buchanan walked along the creek with her as she admired the view of the green garbed mountains.

She said, "I'm quite in love with your country, you know."

"It's a heap o' country."

"England will seem so tiny when we go home."

"Your brother will have his photos."

"Yes. We'll treasure them."

"He's a fight bug, he says."

"Oh, he's quite good at it. He's some kind of amateur champion. He's good at many things."

"He's a nice fella."

They walked and she said, "Could we ride up here? I mean, you do have your horses, you and Coco."

"Coco's horse is a big one."

"Oh, we can ride, y' know. All of us. To the hounds and all that."

"Sidesaddle."

"I can learn the Western way. I want to learn Western ways." Her voice was warm, her eyes glowed. She took Buchanan's arm and turned him back toward the camp. "Let's do. Ride up high among those glorious tall trees."

They walked back. The miners were putting up the sides of the boxing tent. Buchanan watched for a moment, then said, "Afraid I can't leave right now. Coco's about to box. He likes for me to be around."

"Later, then?" She smiled at him.

"Later." He went to the cabin. Coco had donned the long johns he used for training. Buchanan wound his knuckles with soft linen, forming the muffles.

Coco said, "I just hope one of 'em knows what he's doin'."

65

"Uh-huh." He finished tying up the tape.

They went into the fight tent. The duke and his wife and butler and camera were on hand. Lady Caroline smiled at them. Crocker was in the background. The miners appeared, stripped, their muscles bulging, their calloused hands bent from hard labor. Buchanan attended to their muffles.

The duke said, "I say, this is jolly. A bit like home, y' know?"

"Not like home at all," said Lady Caroline. "This is grand. This is beautiful."

"Jolly old England is beautiful," said the duke reproachfully. "Let us not be carried entirely away."

Alex, the biggest one, was ready to go. Buchanan shook his head, sighed. "First you warm up. Shadow box, loosen the muscles."

The three miners obediently began to dance and shove out their fists. They were slow and awkward. Alex favored a wild right-hand swing.

Buchanan said, "The idea is not to kill. Just spar, you know?"

Alex gave him the broad grin that he habitually wore. Coco climbed into the ring. Buchanan followed, his brow creased. Alex stumbled as he went through the ropes. They squared off. Buchanan called, "Time."

Alex promptly reached back and threw the big right hand. The duke shot off his flash. Coco, always gun shy, turned his head at the sound.

The miner's hard fist landed square on the side of Coco's head. The other two miners yipped with glee.

Buchanan jumped forward. Alex was charging the stunned Coco. Buchanan caught him by the arm and swung him around. Still grinning, Alex started another big right hand.

Buchanan ducked and hit Alex in the body with a left. The wind went out of the miner. His two friends jumped into the ring. Everyone was now yelling. Coco stood like an ox, bewildered.

Buchanan seized the two invading miners and yanked their heads together. They went down. Alex lost his grin and came at Buchanan with both hands flailing.

Buchanan hit Alex on the point of the chin, knocking him backwards so that he stumbled over the prone pair and collapsed in a heap. Silence fell like a blanket.

The duke said, "Oh, my. A debacle."

At this juncture Bob Reiner and a few friends arrived at the tent. Buchanan looked down at them. Coco was still trying to shake off the punch he had received.

Buchanan said, "Reiner, take your miners and put 'em back to work. They're useless here."

"But they're strong and willing."

"They're a mess of dead fish," said Buchanan. "Get 'em outa here before I lose my temper."

He went to Coco, whose eyes were glazed. He led him out of the ring and back to their cabin past the wondering stares of the assemblage. His sixth sense had not been wrong. He unwound the muffles and bathed Coco's head in cold water. There was a tap on the door and the duke entered with Lady Caroline and his wife. The duke had a bottle of brandy and the ladies had smelling salts. They hovered, uttering plaintive apologies. Buchanan shook his head.

"This ain't what you might call a good start," he said. "Coco, how you feelin'?"

Coco inhaled the acrid odor of the salts. "Like I been hit by a train."

"What are we going to do now?" asked Caroline. "How can we get sparmates?"

Coco said, "Tom. You done it before."

"Uh-huh." He hated to spar with Coco. In all their long friendship there had been this one thing between them: who was the better fighter? Buchanan had avoided that issue like the plague. He wanted neither to win nor to lose. Now he knew he would have to step in and work out.

The duke said, "I say, for the boxing, y'know. I would be more than happy."

Buchanan regarded him. He was slim and no more than middleweight but he had quickness, perhaps skill. "Uh-huh."

"Oh, sporting," said the duchess.

"Take care of Coco, please." Buchanan went outdoors. Reiner was talking with Crocker.

Crocker said, "Took poor Coco by surprise. Mighta hurt him real bad. Lemme go cook up somethin' for him."

The miners had vanished. Buchanan said to Reiner, "We need sparrin' partners. You set up everything else. How about tryin' to help us out?"

Reiner said in surprise, "But I already tried."

"I see." Buchanan lifted a shoulder. "I'll be ridin' into town with you."

He saddled Nightshade, left word for Coco and went down the steep road to Boulder. He went into the telegraph office. He wrote out a message to Emory. He spoke to the operator, "Friend o' mine name of Highpockets was in here earlier. Tall jasper. You remember who he sent the telegram to?"

"Nope. Lots o' tall fellers around."

"Uh-huh. Be back in a while."

He walked to the hotel and went into the bar. It suddenly occurred to him that he had promised Lady Caroline that he would ride up Boulder Creek with her. He ordered whiskey and pondered. She was the cleverest lady he had known in many a year, maybe ever. She was pretty and smart and agreeable and quick-witted and funny, too, when she wanted to be.

And she was a titled English lady.

He asked the barkeep about Highpockets.

"Sure. Tall, skinny fella. Real interested about the

fight. Wanted to know where the camp was and all. Said he'd be back with a crowd."

"Is he in town still?"

"Took the afternoon train. Said he'd be back, like I told you."

"Uh-huh."

Reiner came into the bar. He said, "It's too damn bad about the sparmates. Sorry about Alex and the boys. They meant well. Best fighters around here."

"Fightin' ain't boxin'," Buchanan told him.

"I just don't know what to tell you."

"I'm tryin' to get help from Emory. Waitin' for an answer to a telegram."

"Y' know we could put up the sides of the boxing tent and charge admission. The kids will want to see Coco train. Come the weekend the college'll turn out. It would help pay the expenses."

"We intend to pay expenses."

"I know. But you were robbed by the Cutlers. If you're a little short it might work out good to have some income."

"That's right nice of you, Reiner. Go ahead with it."

"Uh—you ever meet a lady like the duke's sister?"

"Never did."

"She's really a great one, isn't she?"

"Uh-huh." He was uncomfortable speaking of a lady, in a saloon.

"She sure thinks the world of you."

"Uh-huh."

Reiner said, "Well. Enough said. Got to go up to one of the diggings. See you later."

"Yeah. Thanks again." Extra money would help the present situation. Reiner seemed the right sort, a handsome young man, wealthy, pleasant, open in his manner. He was smitten with Lady Caroline of course. Nothing strange about that. Anyone would be. Buchanan shook himself, had another drink and returned to the telegraph office.

The telegram was of considerable length. He read: "Burgess pulled one hired sparmates from New York and am unable to find others can't you use the miners what is wrong up there I have plenty money coming in here regards to the duke and Reiner hope you can manage town still talking about you and Madame and the robbers. . . . Emory."

The operator said, "Say, Mr. Buchanan, we're all for you up here in Boulder. Anything we can do?"

"Can you box?"

"Me? I couldn't fight a weak cat in an alley."

"You're sure you don't remember my tall, skinny friend?"

"Sorta." He wrinkled his brow. "Seems like he was quittin' a job or somethin'. In Wyoming. Is he a boxer?"

"More like a rat," said Buchanan.

He rode back up the trail. It was late afternoon and above the highest peaks of the mountains thunderheads gathered to match his mood. If Highpockets was quitting Jepson, then what was he doing in Boulder? It didn't make sense. The only thing that did make sense was the shrewdness of that feisty little Burgess in tying up the good sparmates. There weren't many of them in the West at any rate. The best men wouldn't train with Coco or his peers. So Burgess had hired the others.

He rode into the camp. The first thing he saw was Coco's chestnut, saddled and tied to the hitching post. He dismounted and Lady Caroline came from her cabin. She waved and called, "I'm ready. How do I look?"

She was wearing pants unquestionably cut for a boy. Her shirt had probably come from the duke's wardrobe and was tight around the bust. A red silk scarf adorned her slender throat. Her boots were British, low heeled.

He said, "A regular cowgirl. It's pretty late to go into the mountain. See those clouds?"

"You promised." She did not pout, she just looked at him.

"I sure did."

He gave her a hand. She landed neatly in the saddle. He shortened the stirrups and cautioned her. "This horse's gait will be different from what you're used to. And don't pop up and down . . . what do you call it?"

"Posting," she said. "I think I've watched Western riders enough. You grip with your knees and sit tight, what?"

"Somethin' like that." He should have known she would be capable. Nothing seemed to daunt her. "Is Coco okay?"

"Dying to go. Did you have any luck in town?"

"None."

They rode up toward the rippling creek and along its bank. She sat the saddle well enough but not with the natural ease of the Western horsewoman.

He said, "He'll walk but don't hold a tight rein. You neck rein hereabouts." He showed her.

She nodded. She had supreme confidence, he thought. It probably came of being a British lady. Maybe it was just the woman herself. She smiled at him.

He said, "This is somethin' else, you and me ridin' out into what should be a sunset."

"The sun is just behind that peak. Isn't the twilight beautiful?"

"It is." The shades of purple and gray and dark green were somber, he thought. His father had always said that just when things got so bad you couldn't believe they could be worse—then they got rotten.

She said, "You've spoken about many things, Tom. But you never speak about your home."

"Home?" He blinked. "Why, I reckon I don't have a home. Down New Mexico there's a sorta family. Adopted, like."

"Adopted?"

"Well, we adopted each other." He told her about Billy Button and his wife and baby and the gold mine and the long-dead grandfather Mousetrap Mulligan. By the time he had finished they had gone a goodly distance and the clouds had begun swirling around the mountaintops. He said, "We better turn back. It's comin' on rain."

"It's somber. But still lovely." She pulled a little, forgetting to neck rein. The chestnut went obediently toward the stream. It had been raining for some time on high, of course. Now the water came down with the rush of a flash flood.

Darkness came upon them with the suddenness of a black cloud. She gave a little cry. Nightshade stood like a rock but when the thunder and lightning hammered at them the chestnut, restless with a greenhorn aboard, whirled, slipped and slid to the edge of the now-flooding creek. Lady Caroline toppled and fell into the water.

Buchanan thought first of his guns. He stripped them and hung them on the cantle. Then he was down and running.

She did not cry out. She was fighting the current with all her might. The force carried her. She reached for an overhanging branch and missed. Buchanan kicked off his boots and plunged into the water.

The strength of the turbulent creek was like that of a mighty river. He caught up with her in a moment but could not do more than go with the flow. She could swim, he saw that. Another strong branch depended from a creekside tree. She tried for it. She lost balance. Her head struck the branch. She went under.

He reached and grabbed her by the belt. He fought the water with all the power in him. He angled for the bank of the creek. He heard her gasp and thought the icy-cold water had restored her to full consciousness.

His foot struck a boulder imbedded in the creek. He thrust with all his might. He lifted her high and tossed her onto the bank. She rolled over and lay still.

He fought his way out a hundred yards downstream. As was sometimes the way in the mountains, the storm had stopped as abruptly as it had started. He limped back in his stockinged feet to where she sat, her arms propped, her hair down in disarray, the shirt clinging to her wet body so that she seemed, in the dimness, to be naked. She looked up at him.

She said, "That was a go, now, wasn't it, duck?"

He said, "Your head. Let me look."

He felt her scalp. It was not broken, there was merely a lump. She grasped him and pulled herself to her feet, unsteady, clinging to him.

"Tossed me out as though I were a rag doll." She was as calm as a cucumber, he thought. "You're a real Hercules, Tom."

She put her lips up, so that bending over her, his came close. The kiss was as natural as a handclasp. Her hands were on his shoulder, so that they came together, close. Neither wanted to pull away.

Nightshade came trotting to them, nosing at Buchanan. He was not surprised. He was, in a way, rather relieved. The girl laughed and shook herself, spattering wet spray.

Buchanan said, "It ain't to laugh, is it?"

"No," she said. "Not at you."

He went to his saddlebag and brought out a wool

shirt. He put it around her. "Best you don't catch the sniffles."

She buttoned it loosely. She was absolutely unconscious of the exposure of her breasts. "I did a fool thing."

"Never look back," said Buchanan. "Got to get my boots and pick up the chestnut. Got to get you where it's warm and dry."

She said, "You saved my life, y'know."

"A very big thing to save," he said solemnly. "You're a real special lady."

"The Chinese have a philosophy about saving someone's life. You become responsible for that person."

He started to walk, Nightshade following. "If there's one thing you don't need, it's someone to be responsible for you."

"Do tell. Am I then an Amazon?"

"The ladies with one bosom? Couldn't say that."

Now they both laughed. They went arm in arm to retrieve the boots and the horse. It was a free feeling. She was the most attractive woman he had ever met, yet sometimes she seemed like a strong, healthy boy. It was puzzling in one way. In another way it was hugely pleasurable.

It was a gray morning and Boulder Creek still overran its banks. When Coco touched him Buchanan came wide awake, dreams of England evaporated, the blond girl gone from his arms. He growled.

Coco said, "You told me to."

"Uh-huh. You know what? I haven't got any soft shoes for runnin'."

"I got 'em. You can wear mine."

"I hate to run." He pulled on heavy long johns. It was true, Coco's shoes fit him.

"Too much time in the saddle," Coco told him. "You got lard on you."

"Comes of eatin. Man's got to eat."

"No man eats like you, Tom. Come on, now."

They went outdoors. The smell of cooking sent Buchanan into stomach pangs. Out of the adjoining cabin came Bertie Lamb, Duke of Comberland. He wore blue tights and a jersey across which was emblazoned, "Champion of England." He was dancing up and down, beaming. Brister and the duchess bade him stay still as Coco and Buchanan approached. In a moment another photograph went down in history with the flash of powder.

The duke said, "Must keep up, what? Do us all good, a bit of a run."

Buchanan said, "Uh-huh." The duke was slim but finely structured. There were Indians built in this fashion, long, smooth muscles, slim ankles and wrists. They had endurance.

Last night there had been a celebration of the rescue of Lady Caroline, half in fun, half serious. Buchanan could still taste the good whiskey, which now did not have the same flavor. The duke grinned, fresh as a daisy. The duke had endurance.

A rider was coming up the road. Buchanan looked at the slim, trim duke, at the sculptured ebony of Coco, then down at his considerable girth. He cast a quick guilty glance at the windows of the duke's cabin in hopes that Caroline was not watching. He loomed above the others like a granite statue but he did not like the difference.

Bob Reiner drew up a black horse with a white blaze. "Good morning, folks. Afraid I have bad news."

"Burgess hired all the possible sparmates."

"That's right. Bad luck," said Reiner.

"Uh-huh," said Buchanan. He began to trot up the road. "It gets like Pa said."

The duke called, "Sticky wicket, eh? However, onward and upward."

Reiner dismounted and went toward the cook tent.

And thence to Lady Caroline, Buchanan thought. A rich American mine owner and a British lady, a good match according to the newspapers from the East, which occasionally found their way to the frontier.

He was out of breath in less than a mile. The other two pulled ahead. He jogged, uncaring. He was almost down to a walk when he got his second wind. He picked up the pace.

He was never really out of condition. Only a short time before he had been walking the hills and the plains with Coco in search of game. Strength came back to his legs as the results of last night's wassailing wore off. In another hundred yards he had begun to enjoy himself. At the mile he was even with the others.

They ran hard up the last mile. Then Coco turned and they eased down the mountain. The duke was not breathing hard but neither was he as fresh as when he started.

"I say, the altitude, y'know?"

"Uh-huh." Buchanan was saving his breath.

Coco lifted a hand. He was sucking great chestfuls of air. He would have to be able to breathe the mile-high atmosphere of Denver; he meant to be accustomed to it. They came back to the camp in a group. The duke vanished into his cabin, Buchanan and Coco into theirs.

Coco said, "Ten thousand dollars. That's crazy to begin with."

"If Emory sells out that big park he's buildin', the money will be there. Still and all, there's other things. Like you say. Loco."

He was now so hungry he could scarcely wait to change clothing, wash himself down and get to the table. When he got there Lady Caroline and Reiner were in close conversation. It did not detract from his appetite but it didn't make him feel any better.

At two o'clock people began to arrive. Reiner had Alex, still grinning, bearing no malice, and other miners pulling down the sides of the tent, manning a ticket stand made of wooden boxes, collecting fifty cents a head for admission to the show. To Buchanan it seemed a bit cheap but there would be expenses, and his share and Coco's would be enhanced, therefore he forbore comment. He worked on the muffles. Reiner would act as third man in the ring and timekeeper.

Coco and the duke warmed up, then faced each other. Men laughed at the contrast. Someone yelled, "Don't kill the bloomin' duke."

Bertie laughed and put up his hands. Coco moved gingerly, jabbing at the air, dancing. He was amazingly light on his feet. Bertie ducked and came inside and planted two lightning punches to Coco's middle.

Coco's eyes opened wide, then he grinned from ear to ear. The audience began to yell. The two men moved like a brilliant ballet pair, hands flashing. It was the epitome of graceful action. The blows that landed were designedly light, neither intending harm, but they were coordinated. Buchanan caught his breath at the beauty. It was a demonstration of the true art of self-defense.

Reiner blew a whistle. The two men stopped, still moving their feet, keeping warm. All eyes came to rest upon Buchanan.

He felt like a clumsy dolt, climbing into the ring as the duke left, bowing and smiling at the applause. He hated this part of it, he hated the muffles on his hands. He was a free-swinging street and bar fighter par excellence, he was no fancy Dan. He moved well for a man his size but without the swinging grace of the true boxers.

Now Coco's demeanor changed. He came down off

his toes. He lowered his hard head and jabbed with more force. He hooked and struck for the body, holding back very little.

Buchanan caught the blows on his hands and forearms. No one had better reactions than he. While he seemed not to move with speed he was never on target. He moved in and out of Coco's terrain, never trying to throw a punch, always defending.

Coco muttered, "Come at me, Tom. Come at me."

Buchanan shook his head. He was shoving Coco around when needful, making him work. The harder Coco tried, the easier Buchanan outmaneuvered him.

"Hit me," Coco begged.

Buchanan said, "Uh-huh."

Coco made a fast feint and sank a hard right hand to Buchanan's middle. It was a punch hard enough to floor a steer. Buchanan took it and countered reflexively.

The bandaged fist caught Coco alongside the jaw. It sent him floundering backwards. He fell against Reiner. Their feet tangled. Both of them hit the floor of the ring. They lay there a moment in a heap.

Buchanan said, "Just an accident, folks." He tried to separate the two, the muffles interfering. In the interim Coco recovered his senses and leaped to his feet as Buchanan helped the dazed Reiner.

Coco said, "I didn't mean for you to hit me that hard."

"Just a slip," Buchanan assured him. "Let's go at it."

They worked for another round. Then the duke came in again. Alternating, they boxed fifteen rounds. Then Coco put on an exhibition of rope skipping to send the paying customers home happy.

When they had bathed and were gathered, Reiner said, "The word will go out that Buchanan knocked down Coco. I know the Denver gamblers. The odds will change."

Buchanan asked, "And what are the current odds?"

"They were even. Then somehow the word got out about sparring partners, I expect. Ford was favored seven to five. He'll be favored even more after today."

Buchanan said, "I seldom bet. But if you could put up a few thousand for me I'd be obliged."

The duke chimed in, "And a few thousand pounds for me, Bob. I think people are not truly observant."

"What do you mean by that?" asked Reiner.

Coco answered, showing perfect white teeth. "Tom, here, he could whip nine-tenths the boxers in the world if they mixed it with him. What I needs is some hittin' on me. Need to toughen up. Need to get up when I'm down. Me and Tom, we've worked before. He knows what to do."

"Righto," said the duke. "Not observing, y'know. People think they know about boxin'. Seems the most natural sport, what? In many ways 'tis. However."

"And you're the perfect workout for speed," said Buchanan. "Anyone can see why you're a champ."

"Amateur." He seemed a bit wistful.

"But we do need more help," Buchanan said. "The two of us can't do it all. If one of us has an accident, the show's over.

" 'Sufficient unto the day is the evil thereof,' " quoted the duke. "Shall we join the ladies?"

He was a cheerful cuss, Buchanan thought as they went to the cook tent. They seated themselves and Reiner made sure that he was next to Caroline. Buchanan sat across from them and surreptitiously studied their attitude toward one another. Reiner was truly assiduous. Caroline was receptive to a point, smiling, talking in her light, brittle accent. They made a fine, handsome pair—and young, too, younger by far than Buchanan.

Still he ate with the gusto of yore. The food was plain but savory. Coco alone partook lightly. It was odd to be served by Brister under these circumstances, high in the hills, but Buchanan understood protocol. He had, at times, sat with the mighty.

After supper Reiner left. Lady Caroline took Buchanan's arm and urged him toward Boulder Creek. "The scene of the crime," she said. "I'll never forget it."

"The creek's a river now," he replied. "It must still be storming up high."

She stayed close beside him. They stood and listened to the sound of water burbling over rocks. The camp was silent excepting for the sound of dishes being washed by Crocker.

She said, "It's going to be difficult to get Coco into condition, isn't it?"

"We'll do what we can. Bertie is fine."

"But you're betting."

"Reiner told you?"

"He said you are all betting. Is that clever?"

"It's the way we feel." It was hard to explain. "Maybe because it's a tough go. Maybe that makes us feel we got to bet."

"I understand." She hugged his arm. "You are dear people, all of you."

"And I got to be up at five," he said.

They parted with a light kiss. It was becoming a custom for them to kiss, he realized. She tripped away to her tent.

He went to bed and dreamed of tall, skinny men and tough little fight managers and slim blond ladies all mixed together.

5.

Mme. Velvet moved about the gambling room as if on wheels, smiling gravely, bestowing a tap on the shoulder here and there to good customers. At a faro layout there were young Sonny Gilbert and Harry Jackson. Talking with them as they played without much interest was a tall, thin man in cowboy boots, tight jeans, checkered shirt, loose vest. She drifted that way, nodded.

Sonny Gilbert said, "Thanks for the other night, madame."

"Always a way out," she said.

"I should hope so, ma'am. That Buchanan, he's a real home-fried hero, ain't he now?"

"He's been known to do things, they tell me." She noted a disparaging expression that flitted across the hatchet face of the tall man. "This is a friend of yours?"

"Name of Highpockets," said Sonny. "Just passin' through."

"You're welcome here." She gave her standard wave of the hand and moved on. There was something about the new man and the two young Southerners which nagged at her. She gave a signal to the faro dealer and went into her office.

The dealer came in a few moments later. He asked, "Something, madame?"

"The two blond men and the skinny one. What were they talking about?"

"Buchanan, some."

"Anything else?"

"They were askin' questions. Highpockets was answerin'. About the fight, I reckon. The camp up at Boulder, so on. And they don't cotton to Buchanan."

"Those boys he saved from trouble?"

"Reckon they're jealous or somethin'. Highpockets, seems like he's got a grudge. Seems like he's workin' for Gilbert and Jackson now."

"What's their business?"

"Never did know. They ain't been around that long. I thought maybe they come in for the fight."

"Thanks, Bigby. Take a break."

He hesitated. "Can I talk to Maizie?"

"It's against the rules but get her outside. Not too long, now. Get it over and back to work."

They all had a girl. Maizie was a top whore, at that. Bigby had good taste. It was necessary to break a rule once in a while to hold loyalties.

She thought about Buchanan. She had been thinking about Buchanan since the night of the attempted robbery. It had been a long time since a man had so stirred her. Now she had an excuse for seeing him—two excuses in fact. She tapped her perfect white teeth with long fingernails and smiled at herself in a little mirror. They said she was the most beautiful brunette in Denver and that no one could claim her affections, that few dared to try. She loved that reputation. Now she found herself giggling.

It would take a couple of days to make arrangements, get added protection for the hall, buy clothing for outdoors. Meanwhile she would use her connections to check out Gilbert, Jackson and their skinny new playmate.

Mme. Velvet arrived at the Boulder camp in a handsome carriage drawn by matched bays and driven by a uniformed driver. The effect of the driver was somewhat marred by the scars on the burly man's face and a bulge beneath his armpit where he carried his pistol, but the overall impression was very classy, she believed. It was after the noon hour and she had to pay to get into the tent, four bits for herself and the man Grogan.

There were two other women present and she recognized them at once from the publicity in Denver. They were the British gentry and, with the aid of Brister, they were operating the duke's camera. In the ring Buchanan was catching Coco's blows in a huge pillow. Coco was stepping around like a lightweight, snorting and slamming punches that shook even the big man before him, denting the pillow with every fistfull.

Mme. Velvet made her way closer to the ring. She was small but she had a way of getting where she wanted. Her smile was open and innocent even to the men who knew her from Denver.

She spoke to several customers and found herself near a corner of the ring. Buchanan was handing the pillow to the duke. She blinked at the sight of Bertie in his tights. Buchanan was winding his hands with tape.

She looked up at him and called, "Howdy, Mr. Buchanan."

He peered down at her, preoccupied, then grinned and said, "Madame Velvet! Good to see you."

"I must talk to you."

He waved and went out to box with Coco. She kept her eyes on his every move. She saw grace in the two-hundred-and-forty-pound figure, a lightness that amazed and thrilled her. She had refrained from betting on the fight. Now that she saw Coco match Buchanan's strength and skill she began to compute her savings and make an estimate of how much she would wager on Coco to win.

She became aware of Lady Caroline across the ring, also paying strict attention. She saw the blond girl flinch when Buchanan was hit, saw her brighten when he countered with his own punch. She knew all about romance. She had wryly given it up for commerce, but she had kept a part of herself hidden and safe and now she felt a slight pang of jealousy. She had, she freely admitted to herself, marked Buchanan for her own.

Later, meeting him outside his cabin, Grogan lurking nearby, she looked up into his face and fluttered her eyelids. "You have enemies, Mr. Buchanan."

"Tom . . . or plain Buchanan suits me."

"You remember those young men at the poker table when the robbers came in?"

"Sure do. One was handy with a Bowie."

"Sonny Gilbert and Harry Jackson. They don't like you."

"Lots of people don't like me."

"That's hard to believe." Now she dimpled. "However. Do you know a tall, thin man called Highpockets?"

Buchanan's interest sharpened. "What about him?"

"He was with Gilbert and Jackson. My dealer heard them talking about getting you, or something like that."

"Gilbert, Jackson. They're southern boys, ain't they?"

"Yes. There's another one of them. I don't know his name."

"Uh-huh." It seemed impossible. On the other hand a voice spoken through a mask would be different from ... It was possible. Not surely, but probably. "You know about the Cutler cousins?"

She looked at him, startled. "Sure, I do. And I saw Jackson one day with two black fellas. Ducking down a side street one afternoon, I remember. Three and two make five. There's five in the Cutler crowd right?"

Buchanan said, "I'll have to send some telegrams. If they're down here the law's got to know."

She said, "I could give you a ride into town. Got a carriage, just like a lady."

"Madame, anybody says you're not a lady, you send 'em to me."

"They're not likely to say it where I can hear," she told him.

"Uh-huh. I believe you." There was something about her that suited him, something honest and straightforward. "I'll take that ride but not today. Can you stay here overnight? There's an empty cabin."

"If you can put Grogan someplace."

"It can be done." They walked back to the camp. Lady Caroline was waiting. Buchanan said, "Want you to meet each other. Mme. Velvet, Lady Caroline Lamb."

They purred. He apologized and made his way to the cabin where Coco and Reiner were talking together. He told them about the Cutler cousins and Highpockets.

Reiner said, "Highpockets must have thrown in with them in Cheyenne. That would account for all the inside information they had when they held you up."

"Uh-huh. I thought of that," said Buchanan. "The air gets clearer but not any better for us. Like my pa used to say, today is the day you worried about yesterday."

Reiner nodded. "I'll go into town this evening. I know some people in Denver, of course."

"Good." Buchanan watched him leave.

Coco asked, "Is it that you ain't sure about him?"

"I ain't sure about anyone but you and me," said Buchanan. "This is loco time."

"You sure gettin' strong. You like to knock me down again this afternoon. Ladies watchin', that's it."

Buchanan said, "Ladies ain't botherin' me."

"Sho! Bother ain't it."

"Get to bed. Five o'clock's too early for me."

Coco chuckled. They turned in and again Buchanan dreamed, this time of men in masks and young blond men in clown costumes and a small, dark creature that flitted uncertainly on the edge of miasma.

As he slept, Lady Caroline was saying over wine, "Why don't you stay in my cabin, madame? There's an extra bed."

"That's real nice of you." It would also allow the British girl to keep an eye on her, she thought.

"Tell me more about your club," said Caroline.

She told stories. She embroidered on the escapade in which Buchanan had been involved. She told of big wins and big losses at the tables. She did not speak of the whores and pimps who infested Denver's underground.

Then she asked about England and how it felt to be of the peerage. The two women, against their wills, found that they liked one another.

The cold camp in the hills lay on the west side of Boulder Creek. Mining had mainly played out there. The six men sat about and ate cold biscuits and jerky. They had supplies for weeks, ammunition and guns and bedding. They were hidden by trees and sturdy brush and a cleft in a wall of rock but they could easily see the conglomeration below. Cal Cutler had a pair of strong glasses. It was afternoon and they had been watching since Buchanan and Coco's early morning run.

Highpockets said, "Never thought I'd wind up with you jaspers. I been goin' straight so long I forgot how it is."

"You like it," said Cal Cutler.

"It gits to you. I was on the dodge in Texas when I was little more'n a button. It's good to get back."

"You did a good job," said Cal Cutler. "You sure about the bank, now?"

"Just like I told you. I checked out the whole shebang."

"That's right good." He looked at his cousins. They shrugged and winked behind Highpockets's back. Cal Cutler returned to the field glasses. He said, "My, oh, my. Will youall look at that, now?"

"What?"

"Mme. Velvet. The whore is visitin' the big man."

"Madame ain't no whore," said Highpockets. "No more she ain't."

Again the Cutlers exchanged glances. "Suh, where we come from, which is God's own country, Mme. Velvet will always be a whore."

"For sure?" Highpockets was out of his depth. "Reckon everybody to his notions."

"It ain't a notion. It's the livin' truth."

"Okay. If you say so." He could sense an undercurrent and he knew the danger that slept in them.

"Now, you take niggers." The black men seemed not to hear as he went on about the superiority of all whites and the inferiority of all blacks.

Highpockets listened.

Cal Cutler broke off his tirade, "And there is the British lady. Now she *is* a lady. Talkin' to Mme. Velvet just like everything is pure cotton. And Buchanan. You know what? I got to start trainin', just like those rednecks. I got to get in condition."

"You aim to fight Buchanan?"

"It is somethin' I pray for."

"He's beat some powerful men in his time."

"We know the stories."

Highpockets started to go on, then stopped. He had seen Coco and Buchanan in action but he thought he had better hold the speech. He had done his job for the Cutlers, in Cheyenne and Denver and Boulder. He had every right to expect trust and respect. He wasn't getting it. He was not a bright man but he had been around the country. The Cutlers were something different from anything he had experienced.

He had known nothing of the Cutler background. It had all started when Jepson bawled him out for a trifling mistake at roundup time. He had met Cal Cutler later. He knew his days in Wyoming were limited and took on the job of spying without further thought. The reputation of the Cutlers was enough to turn the head of any veteran of the owl-hoot trail.

Now his instinct for self-preservation was taking hold. He had seen Cal Cutler and heard him and it was scary. He studied the man, the unquestioned leader. Cutler was conning the camp below, leaning over a ledge. A slim packet of papers fell unnoticed from his shirt pocket.

Highpockets waited. After another hour had passed, Cutler wearied of looking through the glass. He said, "You got us a hideout, you said. Whereat is it?"

"Up a hundred feet. Worked-out mine shaft. An army couldn't get at you."

Cal Cutler said, "We'll sleep here. Go up come mornin'."

Highpockets did not sleep. He made certain the others did. Then he crawled down and retrieved the fallen papers and hid them deep in a hole he dug with his knife at the edge of camp. He had no idea why he did this, he only knew he needed every bit of ammunition on his side. He was stealthy by nature. He thought he could sooner or later get free or in some way double-cross the gang and make off with the enormous loot they carried in their packs and saddlebags and even in their blankets. There would be more after the raid on the Boulder bank. He tried to feel easy in his mind. He failed.

The ride down the mountain trail was made easy by the comfortable springs of the luxurious carriage. Buchanan had been cajoled into going to town. He thought Reiner would have covered what was necessary about the Cutlers but he was, in truth, already bored by the training routine. He had advised Coco to take it easy, work on his speed with the duke. And he had listened to the siren song of Mme. Velvet, aware that Caroline was not too disturbed by the fact of his excursion. The blond girl was too much for him, he thought, a goal not to be attained even if he strove to that end.

Madame was different. They were as comfortable together as old friends. They regaled each other with stories of the gambling halls, the vagaries of the big town and the little towns they had known.

Buchanan said, "Poker ain't a card game. It's a game of knowin' the other fellers."

"A confidence game," she said. "I agree. I've seen the sharpest players beat by a quiet little man who seldom looked at his hole card."

"Matt Winn?"

"You know Matt?"

"He took from Luke Short."

"You know Luke?" A shadow crossed her face. "I knew him. He's too handsome. And too ready to leave, to run off."

"Old pal of mine," said Buchanan. "Square gambler."

"Oh, sure. Best faro dealer in the country. Hell on gals, though."

"The way I hear, no man gets *you* cryin' for him."

"Oh, I don't cry. I just feel sorrowful. Not for a long time now." She cast a sidelong glance. "Guess I'm ready to fall again."

"Lucky man," said Buchanan.

"He don't know it. Yet."

"You'll let him know." Buchanan laughed, happy to be able to talk freely with this beautiful woman.

Thus they came to the hotel where Reiner awaited them. They ate dinner and drank wine and Reiner reported he had notified the governor, the chief of police in Denver and the federal marshal of the presence of the Cutlers in Colorado.

Buchanan asked, "You think we oughta ask some questions of Jepson in Wyoming?"

"He set Highpockets up and quit without notice. He blamed Highpockets for the fight in the club and he had some suspicions about missing yearlings on the range. It was a long telegram. Jepson doesn't like you, but I doubt he has any connections with the Cutlers."

Buchanan nodded. "Reckon you covered it. No use me comin' down here. But I'm glad I did."

Mme. Velvet said, "Runnin' in the morning is not your style, Buchanan."

"Runnin' any old time is bad for the feet," he said. "Reiner, can you get me back up there in the morning?"

"Sure can. Let's have another bottle, shall we?"

The wine was good, the conversation bright. Reiner sure had an easy way with women, Buchanan saw. He treated Mme. Velvet exactly as he did Lady Caroline. It was the measure of a good man.

The time came to retire. Reiner bade them' good night. Mme. Velvet and Buchanan obtained their keys and went up a flight of stairs. They were in rooms opposite one another.

She lingered as he took the key and unlocked her door. "Thanks. You and Reiner, you sure make a woman feel like a lady."

"If you ain't a lady then I don't know one."

"You know one. A pretty blonde."

"Uh-huh."

"Me, I've been there and back."

"You'll do."

She tilted her face and squinted at him. "You know, I was married once. To a big man, almost as big as you. He got himself killed, the fool."

"Sorry." He felt uncomfortable.

"Never did want to marry again. I'm not too old, you know. Younger than people think."

He said, "Young as a blossom in springtime."

"Talk, talk, nothin' but talk," she murmured, and rose on tiptoes.

He kissed her. She stepped back. Her smile was delicate, her eyelids did their trick. "Big men. Ah, me."

She retreated into her room and softly closed the door. He stood for a moment, a bit stunned, thoroughly puzzled. He had never been really clever with women. He loved them but he could not quite understand them. He went to his room and to bed. This night he slept undisturbed by dreams.

Time tumbled down the torrent of Boulder Creek and the day of the fight loomed. Buchanan had to admit that he had never felt better in his life. Coco had tapered off the last few days. The duke was ecstatic: He had boxed, he had taken pictures galore. Lady Caroline was tanned by the Colorado sun and all the others in the company were fit. A general air of complete enthusiasm had enveloped the company.

Charlie Emory appeared. He was bubbling over with joy. He mopped his balding head and said, "Special trains coming in from all over the country, like I knew they would. People from England, thanks to the duke. People from Mexico, Canada. It's the biggest sportin' event the country has ever seen. Not only the West. The country!"

"The newspapers?" asked Reiner.

"Had to give 'em a hundred seats. New York alone is sendin' twenty. Got the stands built. Tabor helped. He's makin' a mint, too, y'know. They're bettin' millions on the fight; every man, jack and child is bettin'."

"And the odds are on Ford," said Buchanan.

"He's in great shape. That little devil Burgess is braggin' up a storm. He's got all Holladay Street followin' him. All but Mme. Velvet. She's takin' the odds, they say."

Lady Caroline said, "A woman after my own heart. How much have you bet, brother?"

The duke said, "More than we could afford, old girl."

"Good," said she. "Otherwise where's the fun?"

Buchanan asked Reiner, "And the Cutlers?"

"The whole city's been lookin' for them. The governor's got special details out. No sign of 'em."

"They're around," Buchanan said. Every time he thought of them he remembered the humiliation in Cheyenne. Now he also thought of Mme. Velvet's place, where he possibly had been sitting at the table with them. They were smart, much smarter than anyone he had encountered in his adventuring up and down the frontier.

Later he walked for a last time with Caroline. They watched the creek and listened to its song.

They were breaking camp, the training was over, they would spend the last two nights in Boulder.

She said, "It's been a lovely time."

"Uh-huh."

She pressed his arm. "You and Coco, you're a perfect match. Friends. What a wonderful thing to have a friend."

"I'm right sure you got many," he said.

"Oh . . . acquaintances. People one knows. Not true friends."

"Well, you got me and Coco now."

"But England is so far away."

"Distance don't mean so much to us folks."

"I wish I could stay."

"You'd miss your home."

"Would I? It's boring most of the time. Bertie has his duties. I tag along."

It was a brilliant day. The rippling creek reflected the rays of the sun.

She said, "I'll never forget Boulder Creek, the way you tossed me out of it."

Once more it seemed that they should kiss. The last time, Buchanan thought. They would separate when the fight was over. It was a wrench to think of not seeing her, not enjoying her.

"I'm goin' to miss you."

She said, "Tom, I could live in this wonderful country. I could, y'know."

"Maybe. Like they say, it's hardest on dogs and women."

They had reached the caravan which had formed for the trip to Boulder. The tent was down. Despite the cabins the arena looked bare, stripped.

She said, "I could do it. I know I could."

Reiner came toward them saying, "All set. Your carriage awaits, m'lady."

She went with him. Buchanan looked after her, the swinging hips, the erect carriage, her fair hair gleaming. He sighed and mounted Nightshade. Coco pulled alongside on the chestnut.

Coco said, "She's sure one fine lady."

"Uh-huh."

"If a man wanted to settle down."

"Mind your business, Coco. Think about the fight."

"I can think in more'n one direction." He laughed. The wagons creaked, stretching the traces; the journey to town was begun.

Coco said, "I so used to this high air maybe I can't breathe down below."

"You're in the best condition I ever saw you."

"How about you?"

Buchanan patted his middle. "I feel right skinny. Got to admit, it made me feel real good."

They rode ahead of the wagons and carriages. Lady Caroline was riding with Reiner, Buchanan noticed. The duke and duchess and Brister rode with the camera equipment. It all seemed very familiar to Buchanan.

The hotel arrangements had been made by Reiner, as usual. Coco and Buchanan shared a large room overlooking the street. They met the others in the lobby. There would be no liquor for the fighter but the others relaxed over a few bottles. Dinner was gay and fulsome. Coco went to bed early, the others sat and talked among themselves like old friends. It did, indeed, seem a shame to break up such an assemblage of pleasant people.

Buchanan tiptoed into the room at midnight. He opened the window on a quiet Pearl Street. Oil lamps flickered, the sky was moonlit and starry. The peace before the storm, he thought, then realized there was another day before the fight, which would be spent in preliminary publicity, the weigh-in and so forth. He went to bed and slept at once.

* * *

Cal Cutler said, "It must be timed to make the train. But you nigras, you ride into Denver. It's only twenty-five miles."

"Yassuh." They were as obedient as if Abraham Lincoln had never existed.

"Cousins, youall ready?"

"If Highpockets has got it down, we're more'n ready."

They all looked at him in the light of the low fire. They were in the high place. They felt vulnerable. When they went down into the town they would be exposed.

Highpockets said, "I learned this long ago. When I get a good look I can make a map."

"You did make a map." Cal Cutler leaned close over the scrap of paper. "No guards. The back way is not lighted, right?"

"Right."

"You know how to use the dynamite?"

"You know your own selves."

"Just want to make sure, suh."

"I know how to use it."

"Then we ride."

They filed down the mountain. They came into Boulder an hour before the midnight train. The town was quiet. Perhaps a dozen people were astir. They came in the back way and dismounted and the black men took over the horses and began the ride to Denver, leaving the Cutler cousins and Highpockets afoot. That made Highpockets nervous to begin with. He was a horseman; walking was a nuisance and a task. Still, he was in it and he knew there was no way out. He led them to the back door of the bank.

The door was stout and iron-braced. The window was barred. There could be no undue noise. Highpockets worked the hinged edge of the door, loosening it.

The Cutlers had come well-supplied. Each carried

a twelve-inch Bowie. Toby and Stonewall had spent hours honing them. Now they attacked the door-jamb, working as a team. They were very quick and Cutler was very strong. In a short time they had the door cracked so that they could use the short bar which they had brought with them. There were other things in the heavy roll of blanket. When the door gave way Highpockets carried the blanket inside.

The Cutlers replaced the door so that it would appear to be unharmed to anything but the closest inspection. Con Cutler remained outside, several feet from the door, hidden in deepest shadow. He carried a sawed-off shotgun. Cal produced a dark lantern, lit it with a wax taper. He consulted his railroad-man's watch.

"Time's a-wastin'. Get at it, gentlemen."

They were careful with the dynamite. They worked the caps, laid the fuse. Cal Cutler examined the big safe with great care.

"Every one of these has a weak point or two. What you say, Highpockets?"

"The hinges. The bolts are like on the door, around the tumblers of the combination. You sure about the noise?"

The Cutlers set the dynamite. Then they enveloped the safe in the heavy blanket. Cal Cutler stepped back to survey their handiwork, then went to the front of the bank and peered out from behind the drawn curtain and shade.

Chris Cutler asked, "How much you reckon is in there?"

"Couldn't guess," said Highpockets. "I only know people kept comin' in all day makin' deposits."

"Well, Cal gets nervish without somethin' to do. We aim to beat the James boys, y'know that. Every li'l bit helps."

Highpockets said, "I don't figure this to be a li'l bit."

He was growing more nervous every minute. It was not that the Cutlers had been rough on him. It was the way they hung together so tight, talked off by themselves so much. And then they had thrown those funny looks at him. Now he saw them taking the hood-masks from their pockets and putting them over their heads, then replacing their hats. They looked spooky. No one offered him a disguise.

Cal Cutler said, "Coast's clear. Set 'em off."

Highpockets hesitated, then lit the fuses. He stepped back and positioned himself behind a heavy desk. The Cutlers lounged as if disinterested. Spooky, all right, he thought.

The explosion was muffled but it seemed the town could hear it. Highpockets could not keep his eyes off the entrance from the street. The Cutlers tore off the blanket. There was smoke but no flame.

The safe door hung partly open. The Cutlers, moving with great speed, yanked it until they could get their hands inside. They began pulling out bills. They had sacks ready to receive the loot. There was a lot of cash, as Highpockets had predicted. He went forward to help them, exulting in the fact that he had indeed done a good job.

Outside there was a shrill whistle, then a subdued rebel yell. Highpockets froze. The Cutlers calmly stuffed the last of the money into the sacks.

Cal said, "Better run for it."

Highpockets started for the door. He was fully frightened now. His long legs scissored. He had almost made the portal when he felt the stunning impact of a blow in his back. He fell forward on his knees, coughing.

Cal Cutler said, "Y' see, suh, you know us. Can't have anybody around knowin' us, now, can we?"

The Bowie was withdrawn. Highpockets coughed again and saw the blood. He put his index finger in the red stuff and tried to write upon the floor. He managed a scrawled letter. Already he could not see. The point of the blade had struck a vital nerve. He lay there, thinking about it, thinking about his suspicions. For the first time in his life he had been fully correct.

He only hoped someone would get to him before he died and that he would be able to speak. He was, after all, a simple man. He wanted to confess. And he wanted to implicate the Cutler cousins.

They distributed the cash about their persons and tucked away their masks as they headed for the station along the back way. They got there just as the train was pulling out; they boarded it and sat in separate cars, relaxed. They would enjoy the journey to Denver. They had big plans for Denver.

A drunken citizen making his way home over the back yards of Boulder had suspected something when he caught sight of Con Cutler standing guard so close to the bank. By the time he had gathered his wits and awakened the constabulary the train had left the station. It was long after the event that Bob Reiner awakened Buchanan with the news.

At the scene of the crime they found Highpockets dead. Someone had trampled the message he had been trying, dying, to leave behind. Buchanan bent close, oil lamp in hand. He could make out only a scrawled letter *C*.

He put the lamp down and said to Reiner, "Mme. Velvet put Highpockets with the Cutlers."

"Then they've been up here in the hills."

"Uh-huh." It was their eyes he had felt spying. His sixth sense had been right once more.

"Too late to look for the trail."

"Trail out of a town is always right hard to find."

"We can put a hundred men in the hills."

"Come daylight," Buchanan assented.

"Nothing we can do now?"

"Send a telegram to search the last train to Denver."

"The train? You think they'd take the train?"

"I don't put anything past 'em. They're right shrewd."

"Then we might get them."

Buchanan said, "If they ride that train into the station they're not as smart as I think they are. Still, it's a chance."

He did not believe it was a smidgin of a chance. He took a last look at Highpockets, thought of poor Jensen back in Cheyenne. He could easily guess why they had killed the cowman from the Jepson ranch. They never seemed to miss a bet. He wondered what they had up their sleeves for the next job.

The death of Highpockets left the authorities with no clues. The Cutlers had not been identified in Boulder, nor near there. They were the smartest bunch he could ever remember. He went back to the hotel. Coco was awake.

When he heard the news Coco said, "You goin' up there tomorrow?"

"We got a day."

"You sorta got to, don't you?"

"Uh-huh."

"You'll be in Denver in time for the fight." It was a statement, not a question.

"Uh-huh."

"Git your sleep," said Coco. "I can take care of myself 'til you get there."

"I know you can."

He did sleep. He also arose before sunrise. He saddled Nightshade and rode up to the deserted campsite and began to think, trying hard to put himself in the place of the Cutler cousins. He had dealt with so many criminal minds in his time that he felt that he could follow their thinking. These men were smarter, more coldblooded and merciless

99

than the others. Still, they had to have plans, they had to have a base of operations. He scanned the mountainside.

Reiner, true to his word, had men of all descriptions climbing and searching. Buchanan retrieved his old field glasses from his saddlebag and stood at a central spot in the camp. The Cutlers would have been spying, therefore they must have been in range of the camp from a definite point of the compass.

He made a mental note of possible spots and mounted Nightshade. The big black horse went up the mountains with seemingly no more effort than it would take to cover level ground.

He stopped several times to turn the glasses down on the camp. None gave a full view. He dropped the reins, loosened the bit and allowed Nightshade to wander at the edge of a now-calm and clear Boulder Creek. He went on afoot.

It took him several hours. Men were scrambling on the opposite hills, Reiner giving orders. The search was being made with great care but, Buchanan thought, not quite in the right direction. The place had to be where no mine was in operation.

At last he found traces of a cold camp. "No sign of a duck's egg," he muttered.

He painstakingly examined every foot of the place. Men had been there. Horses had been there. He picked up faint tracks and estimated there had been six in the party. That accounted for the Cutler cousins, the two black men . . . and Highpockets?

Most likely it was Highpockets. He squatted down and with his knife turned over a small pile of ashes. He kept his attention close to the ground and began to search every foot of the surroundings.

That was how he discovered the buried pad of paper. It was wrinkled and soiled and dampness had softened it. He assembled it with great care. He sat down on a large flat rock and read. The handwriting was sharp and legible, the language that of an educated man. It seemed to begin with a letter to a female.

Dear Essie Lou:

It has been a long time but I love you as much as ever. The road has been hard and the task enormous. But we are succeeding. I cannot send you all the details but we are piling up the money necessary to buy the plantation and start life over again.

We have two niggers who will come back with us, God willing, to begin the work of restoring the plantation. They are Stonewall and Toby. You remember them. All we need now is one more strike and we'll be on our way. We have been very lucky in hitting pay dirt. The money is in a safe place. I also found some fine jewels for your fair throat and beautiful slender wrists. I cannot wait to place them upon you, the fairest flower of the South, my darling. . . .

Buchanan reread it. He shook his head. He picked another sheet of the paper.

"The goddam Yankees put us down but we will rise again. We will beat the James boys and their gang before we finish. Me and my cousins will triumph, we will call in friends and work slow. We are young enough and smart enough to outdo Jeff Davis, who was a fool. . . ."

Neither of the writings was finished. There was room on each page but evidently the thoughts of the writer had gone no further. Cal Cutler, the leader, had written them, Buchanan thought. It fit with his style.

Another page was crowded with figures, dollar

signs. The amounts were large, in the thousands, but again there was no final sum.

The next page was scribbled and Buchanan's name leaped from it.

> We had to kill that man in Cheyenne. We had to kill him because Buchanan, that Texas bastard, would have been on us with his hidey gun. Buchanan is the devil incarnate. Texas is not part of the South and never will be. Buchanan could never be a Southern gentleman. I would give a lot to be able to meet him face to face, unarmed, just the two of us with our bare fists. No Texan can ever stand up in a fair fight with a Southron gentleman.

"Well, at least he finished that one," Buchanan said aloud. "Wonder if it was my fault he killed Highpockets. This gent talks a huge heap. Reckon he believes it when he's sayin' it or puttin' it down on paper. But there's somethin' wrong in his head. Sure as shootin', he's got a screw loose some place. The South'll rise again? I sure feel sorry for poor Essie Lou."

He folded the papers and put them away for future scrutiny. He cast around for track, found traces leading upward. There would be a place there. They would have a secure place.

On the other hand no place in the mountains could be safe forever. There was the matter of provisions. Manpower could surround any one of the hideouts and starve out the people. However, if there was a way out and they could hole up, then escape—say through a pass unknown to Reiner or his men—that would ensure a long chase.

A glance at the sun told him he must go back to town and catch the train for Denver. He would have preferred to check the terrain, but there was no time. He rode down the bank of Boulder Creek admiring the green, the rolling high place, thinking how it must have been before the mining, when the Arapahoe dwelt in this natural paradise.

He thought of his walks with Lady Caroline. The creek was now running in demure fashion, singing a gay song. He did not know what to think about the British girl, he admitted to himself. Their communion had been perfect but there was the fact of the distance between them, geographically at least.

Then he had a quick thought of Mme. Velvet, her open admiration, her quick, wide smile, the beauty of her small body, the shrewdness of her mind. He shook his head and set Nightshade to a smooth pace going down to talk to Reiner.

6.

On the street outside the station Buchanan stood
staring. There had never been so many people in
Denver. He was wearing his city clothing and
carrying his bedroll containing changes and his
six-guns. People swarmed, people of all ages and
description. The flash girls worked the crowd like
vendors. There were no carriages for hire. The
noise was horrendous. He resigned himself to a
walk, shouldering his way, towering above the mul-
titude.

A voice called, "Buchanan! Over here."

A carriage threaded its way through the crowd.
Grogan held the reins, Mme. Velvet waved from the
leather seat.

Buchanan said, "What are you doin' here, lady?"

She said, "We met the early train. They told us
when you'd be arrivin'. Hop in."

He sat beside her. "Now, this is mighty thoughtful
of you."

"We were scared you might get your pocket picked." She wrinkled her dainty nose at him. "The city's full of dips. The coppers are goin' wild."

"The whole town appears to be goin' wild."

"Biggest thing ever to hit town. Want to see the fight arena, as Charlie Emory calls it?"

"Might's well."

Grogan drove through the clatter and clutter, cursing under his breath. People scuttled beneath the snorting nostrils of the team. Urchins ran shouting at everything and nothing. Dogs yawped, vendors howled their wares. Confusion reigned.

Buchanan said, "Looks like a mighty big circus is in town."

"The biggest," she said. "I saw Coco. He looks fine. The duke is takin' pictures of everything that don't move. Charlie Emory's in seventh heaven."

They chatted easily, comfortable in each other's company. He told her about the Cutlers. She nodded.

"Crazy Southerners. The West is full of 'em. They was wronged. All that."

"They got beat," said Buchanan. "But the Cutlers, the way they go about it, that won't do it."

"They're stealin' the country blind. I'd be scared of them, believe me. Real scared."

They came to the east of town. The stark unpainted bleachers could be seen from a distance. Buchanan frowned.

"Green timber. Two by fours and furrin' lath."

"Tabor and his money. And others. You know how many it'll seat?"

"Couldn't guess."

"Near thirty thousand."

"A good wind and a storm and they could be killed."

"At an average of ten dollars per seat," she said. "Thirty thousand. Three hundred thousand dollars. And you thought the *purse* was somethin' big."

"Expenses," Buchanan said. "Still and all. Three hundred is a heap o' thousands. Sure is the biggest show ever to hit the West."

There was a kiosk within which a man sweated in the sun as a serpentine line of ticket buyers moved slowly toward him. The sound of hammers and saws bespoke the fact that all the work on the arena was not completed. Charlie Emory came, wiping sweat from his bald head as they stopped close to an entry gate.

"You see? You see? Can you believe it?" He waved short arms, beaming. "Got the police comin' to handle the crowd."

Buchanan said, "Uh-huh. How's Dan Ford doin'?"

"Coco better watch out. He's in terrific shape. I tell you, for a big man he's quick. Quick as a cat." He made a wide gesture. "If it wasn't for that manager of his. Now he wants more money. Says we're swindlin' him. But Ford's a man of his word. He'll be on deck tomorrow, never you fear."

Mme. Velvet asked, "All right if we go inside?"

Emory yelled at an armed man at the entrance, "These people are okay. Now I got to run. See you at the hotel."

They went through the entry. Mme. Velvet strolled down to ringside and said, "My box is here. The duke's is right next door. How do you like that?"

"Ringside. Musta cost you somethin'."

"Nothin's too good for my people. Of course the ladies of society won't be here. Tried to stop the fight. But the duke's ladies will be here. Along with mine. Is that a joke?"

Buchanan didn't answer. He was looking past the top of the arena to the clouds. There were always a few thunderheads. He wondered now if they would combine to shower down a storm.

Back outside the arena they saw a man with a

rifle leave the kiosk, carrying a sack. He walked a dozen yards to a square building marked "Office." There he was met by another armed guard, who took the package indoors.

"The take," said Mme. Velvet. "Charlie had to hire guns to guard the take."

"Uh-huh," said Buchanan. "He better get it to the bank in a hurry and put extra people guardin' the bank. The Cutlers are loose and they ain't the only thieves in Colorado."

They returned to the carriage. Grogan was talking with an acquaintance. Madame asked, "You want to go to the hotel? Or would you rather come down to my place?"

"Coco's waitin' at the hotel. Not that I don't appreciate the offer."

She gave him one of her upward swinging looks complete with a *gamine* grin. "Any time, Buchanan, any time."

She was indeed good company. She pointed out the opera house, told a tale about Baby Doe Tabor, confessed that her business had been so profitable that she was thinking of closing down.

"I could disappear, turn up some place else and be a real lady. Maybe in another year I'll do just that."

"And quit gamblin'?"

Her face clouded. "The gamblin' is okay if you're on the square like your friend Luke Short. Even for a woman in the West. There's been others besides me. It's the other part I don't cotton to."

"Without the gals you're out of business."

"Don't I know it?" She looked straight at him. "I was never in that. I was never a hooker."

He was embarrassed. "Never believed you were."

"I was married. I been in love. That's it."

"Uh-huh."

"People will tell you different. Now that you been seen with me, there's plenty will lie to you."

"Never believe anything you hear and only half what you see," said Buchanan.

"Just wanted to get it straight."

They had arrived at the hotel. Buchanan shouldered his blanket roll. He said, "I thank you kindly. I'll be seein' you after the fight."

"Maybe."

"What do you mean, maybe?"

"There's the duke and the blonde." She grinned again. "Hoo-eee. You can't fool a veteran, Buchanan."

Grogan drove her away. He looked after the carriage, thinking what fun she was and how acute, and that in other circumstances, at another time and place . . .

He broke off and went into the hotel. Newspapermen rushed to him. He stood and looked down at them and patiently answered questions until repetition roiled his mind. Then he got the key and went up to his room.

Coco was stretched on a bed. He was reading one of the local newspapers. He said, "You know what? We the biggest thing this side of Dan Ford and that Burgess man. We bigger'n Texas."

There was a clever drawing of Coco and Ford and Burgess on the front page. There was also a long story about the coming bout and Buchanan, "the famed frontiersman."

"Says here you kilt twenty men in fair fight. Don't say how many you let off."

Buchanan said, "They don't count too good, do they?" He went to wash up. "You behavin'? You eatin' right?"

"Yeah, the duke's been takin' over, sorta. He's bringin' that camera to the fight. Never seen a man more excited. The ladies in town think it's awful that Caroline and the duchess are attendin'."

"And Mme. Velvet."

"They say plenty about her. This here's a kinda scary thing, ain't it, Tom? All the fuss, all the money, all them people comin' from every place."

"You just worry about Dan Ford."

"I worryin'. Not much. But a little bit. Reckon he's the best I ever met."

"No man can whip you," Buchanan told him. "You're the best. Just believe that."

"I got to believe it. Guess whilst you're in my corner it might be true."

They went down to dinner in a small private room where the duke and his party awaited them and Brister poured wine. People tried to intrude and were unceremoniously rebuffed by tough-looking men dressed in formal clothing that did not become them. Buchanan remarked that Coco was right, it was bigger than Texas—or at least any sporting event that had ever taken place in Texas or anywhere else in the West.

The duke said, "And I'm photographing it all. Imagine what my friends back home will say!"

Caroline said sweetly, "You didn't know it but we got a picture of you and Mme. Velvet when you descended from her carriage. We looked for you at the station but you had gone."

"Didn't see you. She was waitin' for me."

"Thoughtful of her. She's quite a dear, isn't she, now?"

"Uh-huh." Buchanan retreated into his dinner.

They retired early against the excitement of the coming day. Lady Caroline had little more to say to Buchanan. He felt uncomfortable. He tossed and turned, feeling the excitement over and above any other emotion. He slept uneasily.

Mme. Velvet was half asleep, thinking of Buchanan, thinking of her youth in Kansas, when her name

110

had been Louise Lee Gilbert. Her mother had been a strong lady with a weak body. Her father had been a gambler and a dandy. Her cousins had been farm boys and it was they who forcibly taught her about life—and death.

She had killed Rafe, the one who raped her. She had run away. She had adventured on the river. She had used the tricks her father taught her from the time she could talk, and she had become notorious and had taken the name "Mme. Velvet."

There had been her first husband, who died untimely because he forgot her stern admonition not to use holdouts in a poker game. There had been others, two of them. Now for a long time there had been nobody, until she met Buchanan.

The curtain of her second-floor bedroom above the gaming hall swung sharply in a sudden cool breeze. She went to the window and saw that the sky was black. She was about to close the window when a large, strong hand closed over her mouth.

"Buchanan?" she gasped.

The word was indistinguishable. A man came gracefully over the sill and into the room without relinquishing his grasp. He was as big as Buchanan, slimmer perhaps, and masked. Then she knew it was Cal Cutler.

He said, "No noise, please, ma'am. I will not harm you in any way if you make no noise. Promise?"

She managed to nod. There was a guard close to her door but she knew better than to call out. The hand came away and produced a gun.

"Sorry, ma'am, but I know you. I must ask you to get dressed. If you got pants, better put 'em on. It'd work out for decency and all."

"Dress? Whatever for? The money's all in the bank. I don't wear jewels, they're in the vault."

"It ain't your money we're after," he said politely. "It's your own self, ma'am."

"Me? What in the hell for?"

"You heard of insurance? What they're sellin' now, that new thing. Life insurance, they call it. You're to be our insurance."

She recognized at once what it meant. She remembered how Buchanan had spoken of these men, that they would kill anyone who opposed them. She drew in a breath and said, "You're goin' to watch me dress?"

"Wouldn't take an eye off you. No offense intended, ma'am. We ain't that kind of folks. We're Southrons."

"North, south, east, west," she muttered. "Men!"

Nevertheless she removed her nightgown without flinching. She found her riding breeches and boots and a chemise and a woolen shirt and donned them under his dispassionate eye. He was, she decided, a queer one. He neither flinched nor flushed, merely watched her to make sure she didn't have a hidden gun in the room.

He said, "Have to ask you to go down the ladder, ma'am. Don't expect you're scared, though. You're not the scary kind."

The ladder was sturdy. She went slowly down to where two others waited. It was the fight gate, she thought. It had to be the huge amount that would be taken in tomorrow. Not all of it because some was in the banks, but enough to tempt the Cutler cousins.

She wondered who would die this time. Her own chances were not good. Buchanan—they hated Buchanan and he would be first choice when the showdown came. There would be a showdown. She was sure of that.

Two of the men shouldered the ladder. The big one kept a firm grip on her arm but without bruising her. They went the back way and deposited the ladder between two houses. They removed their masks.

"Sonny Gilbert and Harry Jackson, at your service, ma'am. And this is Randolph Parkhill."

"So you say." She shrugged.

"By those names ye shall know us," cautioned the big one, who had to be Cal Cutler. "I told you that we wish you no harm. On the other hand, there could come a time. Remember, we helped save you once."

"You and Buchanan."

Even in the pitch darkness she could feel him stiffen. He said, "Stay close and make no sound. None, you heah me?"

She obeyed. In their quiet politeness there was a deadly note. She was brave, she had been through scrapes in many a hot spot, but now she felt the coldest danger.

They knew the back streets far better than she did. They moved with confidence. They came to an unpretentious house on a street she did not recognize and went indoors.

Cal Cutler said, "This is Mme. Velvet . . . Rosalie Hightower."

The lady was of no particular color or description. She smiled at Cal Cutler and said, "Any friend of yours."

"She stays in her room until we need her."

"If you say so, darlin'."

Two black men entered, stared hard at Mme. Velvet, departed.

Cal Cutler said, "Like I say, we won't harm you. But the blacks, you understand, they could be out of control if you made a fuss. Only you ain't to make a fuss, are you, ma'am?"

"No," she said. "I ain't about to make a fuss."

The room was neat and clean. It contained a single bed, a dresser, a commode. Dainty curtains were at the window. A Georgia landscape was on the wall. She had, she thought, been captured and transferred to the Deep South.

They left her. She sat on the bed. They had plans and no one had to tell her they were carefully laid and that she was part of them. She was a hostage.

She thought of Buchanan. He would miss her at the fight. There was no possible way he could leave to search for her even if he were so inclined. Her own people would report that she was missing but the state of the populace, the scattering of the police would prevent any real action on her behalf.

She said, "Louise Lee, you are in a picklement."

There was no time or inclination for tears. She stretched out on the bed and tried to sleep. She removed nothing but her boots. Tomorrow, she thought; there was going to be a hell of a tomorrow.

And she would miss the big fight. One tear escaped because she would miss the big fight.

In the morning the dawn was uncertain. Running around the block with Coco to loosen the muscles Buchanan cast glances at the sky. He did not like what he saw.

On 18th Street they came face to face with big Dan Ford and Tony Burgess. They paused. No reporters were in view.

Burgess snarled, "Been duckin' us, have ye? Scoffin' with the duke and them. Lettin' a bank be robbed. What kind o' people am I scummed up with? Cheatin' us outa a million dollars. Bad cess to ya all."

Ford asked, "How do you feel, Coco? Everything good for you?"

"Just fine," said Coco, prancing in place.

"Looks like rain."

"Can't tell in this country," said Coco. "Hey, good luck to you."

"I'm ready," said Ford, showing his gold teeth.

"He'll beat your ass off," said Burgess. "Now think o' that, me buckeroos. Dan'll knock ya to smithereens."

"We're scared to death," said Buchanan. "Why don't you get your fine man ready and stop the nonsense?"

"Don't gimme none of your guff," said Burgess. "If I was half your size I'd take ya on meself."

Ford gave him a playful push. "You wouldn't believe it, but he's got a wife and five kids back home. G'wan, Tony, run it off. See you this afternoon, fellas."

They continued to run. Coco said, "It does look like rain. Muddy turf. I don't near-cotton to muddy turf."

"Play it like it lays," said Buchanan. "Let's go around to the hotel and eat."

In their room the ebullient Maureen O'Dea served them steak and eggs and biscuits and honey and quarts of milk. They would not eat again until nightfall. Coco ate slowly, his brow furrowed.

"You worried about somethin'?" asked Buchanan.

"Just that everything ain't been goin' so good. Them Cutlers. No sparrin' mates. And I scared of that grandstand. It looks shaky to me. And then the rain. Bad-luck signs, Tom."

"You don't believe in such."

"True, I don't. Not usual. But this here. I dunno."

"Look, Coco. You make the fight. You do the best you can. Angels can't do no more."

"All them people bettin' their shirts. All that money. And them Cutlers runnin' around loose."

"We'll deal with the Cutlers later." He had a hunch about the mountains above Boulder. "When the fight's over." There was a tap at the door. The duke entered. He beamed upon them. "Clouds cannot dim our victory. Cheer up, my boys, it's a day for the game."

"Uh-huh," said Buchanan. "We've got to thank you for all you've done."

"Speeded me up no end," said Coco. "Like fightin' a butterfly, only more fun."

"Worryin' a bit about the camera, you know. But we can get pictures in darkness, nearly. Sure you don't need me in the corner?"

"Tom handles me. I feel better just with him."

"Good-o. I'll just shove along, then. Want to get the early arrivals, the preliminary bouts. What a show I shall put on at home!"

"You'll be leavin' directly after the fight?" asked Buchanan.

"Unless somethin' jolly excitin' happens. If I could get a picture of those Cutlers, now."

Buchanan said, "They might be holed up in the hills. I got a notion about them."

"If so, I'll be there. Good luck, my friends. Best o' luck."

He was gone, blithe as a morning lark. Maureen came in and began to gather the dishes.

She said, "You wouldn't believe it. The duke asked me to go to the fight. Sit in the royal box. Lawsy me."

"Take a slicker," Buchanan advised her. "It may rain on you."

"Rain, shine, snow or hail. I'll be there. With me last dollar bet on Coco, ye think I'd miss it? Oh, la, la."

Coco said, "All the poor people, all the blacks, they bettin' on me. And it comes mud anybody can slip and lose."

Buchanan said, "I've got your cleated shoes in the bag. Never did see you worry about a fight."

"It ain't Dan Ford that buggers my head."

"Uh-huh. That satisfies me," said Buchanan. "Now, you go put down your head until I come for you. And let the good thoughts run free."

He left the room. Coco would rest, probably sleep. He had inner strength that always came through for him.

Downstairs was a madhouse. People were up and around, gamblers were placing their bets. The ladies were holding meetings, outraged at the idea of the prize fight taking so much of the town's interest and time. The police were sweating out an attempt to keep order. Liquor was flowing—already a ban had been put upon drinking at the event.

Lady Caroline seemed to swim on the surface of it all. She led Buchanan to the small private dining room. "What is this I hear from Bertie about the Cutlers and the mountains?"

"I got hold of some papers." He told her about them. "I think they've stashed loot up there. They wouldn't trust banks. They're smart enough to find a place that would be safe for a bit of time."

"Why haven't they gone away?"

"That's the question," said Buchanan. "I got to warn Emory and the police. I believe they're still around Denver, where all the money is at. It just makes sense they wouldn't walk away from a gold mine."

"So Bertie says. Then he'll be there with his bloody camera." She smiled. "Such language! Pardon me. But I shall be there, also. I haven't had a chance to talk with you since those walks along the creek."

"It's been busy. I miss you, too."

"I wish I could persuade you to come to England with us. For a visit. Would it not be pleasant?"

"Me! England?" He was surprised how shocked he was at the idea.

"We have hunting also. And riding."

"On one of them funny saddles?" He laughed.

"You could bring your own. You could bring Nightshade aboard ship."

"Nightshade wouldn't like it," he told her. "I been to New York, Chicago, St. Louis. Strange places east of the Rockies ain't for me. I just don't breathe well."

"I was afraid of that."

He touched her hand. "Maybe you could come back here. Bertie seems to like it here."

"He adores it. And so do I. But we do have duties, you see. Bertie sits in Parliament. There are . . . oh, things."

"Uh-huh." The gap between them had never been wider. He could not visualize the "things" but he could imagine pomp and circumstance.

She said, "Oh, Tom, I don't know how I shall do without you, really I don't."

And then they were kissing again. Her lips were soft and moist. Buchanan had to set her away lest someone come in upon them.

"You're the finest lady I ever knew," he told her.

"You're the only man I ever . . . ever really wanted to kiss." She did not blush, she looked him in the eye.

He said, "I think we better mosey along. I think I'm scared."

"The great Buchanan scared of a slip of an English girl?"

He said soberly, "Not of you, lassie. Of me."

Now she did flush. They went out among the people and she found her brother, the duchess and Brister. She waved once as they departed so that they could be early for the picture-taking. Bob Reiner joined them as they left. Buchanan sighed and went back to the reporters and the crowd and the bettors. He found a place at the far end of the bar and drank a double whiskey. He felt better when he went back upstairs.

There was a carriage to take them to the arena. The streets had been full for days and now people streamed toward the scene of the fight. They were met by Charlie Emory, bursting with excitement and joy. He showed them to a makeshift dressing room beneath the stands just as a preliminary boxer was being brought in half conscious on a stretcher.

Coco asked, "He get beat by the fighter from Ford's dressin' room? That's bad luck."

"Forget it," said Emory. This is the greatest show ever. There's more money in my office safe than I ever expected to see. We got Honest John Daley to referee your fight. The great Daley."

"The great Frisco drunk," said Buchanan. You sure he's sober?"

"As a judge."

"Not like some judges I know, let's hope." He was nervous. Coco was moodily surveying the beaten boxer. "How many more bouts?"

"Just one," said Emory. "Got to run, now. Good luck."

"I bet he said the same to Ford," said Coco.

"The man's excited. He did put it on, the big fight."

"Just so he gets our money up."

"You heard him, plenty of money. Get up and move around. Work up a sweat."

Coco obeyed. Time dragged like a plow in rocky soil. Buchanan arranged the pail and water bottle filled at the hotel. He put smelling salts in his vest pocket, took them out and went to the dazed gladiator. The man sniffed, wiped away dried blood and stood up.

"Thanks, Buchanan."

"Tough goin' in there?"

"Too tough." He spat. "Name of Holley. I was sparmate to Ford. He's mighty good. Took a lot outa me, boxing with him. He hits a ton."

Buchanan said, "We know."

"You want me in your corner, be glad to oblige."

Buchanan said, "I work the corner. But you could help with the pail and stuff."

"Like to see Coco beat him. Nice man, Ford, but that Burgess is a bastid."

They waited. The crowd roared. Flies buzzed. The air was close and damp. Buchanan went out and looked at the sky. It was worse than before. Inwardly he groaned. Coco disliked fighting in the rain.

The call came at long last. Coco donned his royal-blue robe over tights of the same hue. He was sweating nicely, Buchanan thought. His eyes were clear and now his concentration was wholly on the job before him. He was, first and last, a champion fighter; it was in his heart and soul.

Holley carried the bucket and four policemen escorted them to the turf where the ring had been laid out. Honest John Daley, a barrel-chested veteran, awaited them. Charlie Emory was standing at ring center, megaphone in hand.

The crowd roared. Ford, Burgess and a handler came to the opposite corner. Again the cheers rose to the leaden sky.

Charlie Emory began his introductions. "In this box, ladeez and gemmun, we have most distinguished visitors from our cousin country across the sea . . . the Duke and Duchess of Comberland and party."

There were a few boos and a mighty yell of approval. Buchanan saw Caroline waving a red and white handkerchief. He gestured toward her and her family.

He looked for Mme. Velvet in the adjoining box. There were several of the girls from the gaming house. There was her second in command, Bigby, who looked worried, gesturing toward an empty seat, then to Buchanan.

Emory was saying, "This-here bout is for the champeenship of the West. . . . These two men are the best who ever met this side of the wide Mississippi.

The winner will challenge the champeen of the world. . . ."

Mme. Velvet would not have missed it for all the money on Holladay Street, Buchanan knew. There was no possible opportunity to talk to her employee. He could not leave the corner for an instant for fear of upsetting Coco. He wondered if she had been stricken ill. The thought disturbed him more than he liked.

Honest John was coming to ring center. Emory had about finished. There was nothing to do but go on with the proceedings. Buchanan walked with Coco, forcing himself to pay strict attention to what was happening.

Emory introduced the referee and ducked out of the ring. The stage was set.

Honest John Daley had bulging eyes and a red, veined nose. He beckoned and they met in the center of the ring, Burgess and Ford, Buchanan and Coco. Emory called for them to pose and they waited until the flash of magnesium told them the duke had his photograph. Again Buchanan looked for Mme. Velvet. It was reflex; his eyes returned at once to the referee.

"Yez know the rules. London Prizefight. No dirty business, now. Go to your corner and come out fightin'."

Dan Ford wore white. His body was tanned by the Colorado sun, and he was trim. His muscles were smooth and long, as were Coco's—the structure of the trained boxer. He smiled, waved, then was serious. Coco responded without change of expression.

The timekeeper said, "Time, gentlemen."

They came to the mark at ring center. Ford was a standup boxer, his fists poised. Coco crouched, holding his hands closer together, ready to hook or cross with either. They sparred a moment.

Ford led with a lightning left. It caught Coco by surprise. He went down more from shock than anything else. Buchanan leaped forward and brought him to the corner for the required thirty seconds under the rules.

Coco said, "Well, they done said he was quick."

"No power in that one."

"Time," came the call.

Coco danced out. The sky was still overcast, the rumble of the crowd nearby yet remote to the ears of the combatants and their corners. Again they sparred, then Coco went on close and drove a flurry of punches to the body. Ford retreated, his smile evaporated.

Out of the crouch Coco threw a right cross. It struck Ford's jaw and the bigger man reeled into his corner. He swayed, then fell. Burgess, snarling, cursing, ran to him.

Buchanan said, "Try him with the left. Set him up."

"I'm tryin' him with everything I got, every which of a way."

They went to the mark again. Coco danced. Now he was quicker than Ford. The big man had taken too much punishment. They exchanged lefts. They missed with rights. Ford came close and tried to wrestle Coco to the ground. Coco squirmed loose and drove heavy blows to the body, one, two, three, four.

Ford gasped, recovered and shot a desperate right hand to the temple. Coco went down once more.

In the corner Buchanan said, "This has got to stop. You never have been down twice in a fight before now."

"The man's got hand speed. His feet's slow but his hands, they're damn quick."

"You put him down once. First time ever, they say. Try it again." He was keeping it light even as he worried.

122

Again they went at each other. Ford's fists flicked out, a good one-two glancing off Coco's guard. Coco retreated. Ford rushed. Coco sidestepped. He hooked to the nose and blood spurted. He dropped another punch to the body. Ford's defense came down. Coco blasted a right cross to the jaw.

Ford fell hard. Burgess and his helper had to drag him to the corner. The crowd set up a howl to the darkened skies.

Coco stood with Buchanan. "Never hit a man harder. And look at him."

Ford was blinking and nodding as Burgess wildly gave instructions. He seemed far more placid than the weather. There were clouds like huge vultures over the scene. The duke took another picture.

Buchanan said to Holley, "Keep the towels dry. Wrap them under your shirt, anything."

Coco said, "I hates the rain."

"Time."

Coco went out fast. Ford met him. They traded punches to the body, to the head. Each refused to go down. Blood began to flow from cuts. The mob was howling its head off for sudden death, each according to his bets.

The deluge came. Coco slipped and almost went down. It thundered. Lightning sent its zigzag message across the skies. The women from Mme. Velvet's place uttered little screams as their finery drooped. The duke and his party donned the slickers with which they had come prepared. Few left the arena as the two giants battled.

Coco almost fell. Ford struck a hard right which, fortunately, brought him erect. Coco jabbed three times. Ford was quick, but not quick enough. Coco was measuring him, timing his punches. They staggered around and around as the turf quickly became slippery. Coco threw a long right hand. It landed on Ford's chin.

Ford went down with his legs crossed like a hog on ice. Burgess and the other second rushed to drag him to the corner.

Buchanan said, "That would've done it except for the footin'."

"Landed square." Coco was watching across the puddles which had immediately cluttered the dirt of the ring. "Damn mud."

The duke's party was on foot, leaning. Brister was protecting the camera. The rain pelted them. Lady Caroline was calling something but Buchanan could not distinguish her words.

"Time," came the call inexorably.

Coco shuffled out, trying the footing. The mud came to his ankles, so heavy was the downpour. He waded through it.

Ford came to the mark. He led with his rapid left. Coco planted his feet and dodged. Ford tried a right cross. Coco picked it off, then shot his left to the nose. Ford's eyes watered. Coco repeated the move, dropped a hard right to the body. Ford's speed was lagging.

Coco jabbed, then hooked off the jab. He caught Ford leaning in the wrong direction. Ford began to collapse at the knees. The thunder and lightning lent fury to the scene. Buckets of water came down.

Coco refused to try to move his feet. He lowered his head and punched, right, left, right, left. The big man opposite him came slowly apart.

Ford fought back. Coco took his blows. Ford tried a mighty uppercut. Coco withdrew his chin and leveled a driving right fist.

Ford did not drop. He seemed to come apart, section by section, first his ankles, then his knees, then his hips, then his torso. He collapsed into a heap.

Burgess and the second came running, knelt, the rain steaming their clothing, running into their eyes. Burgess looked at the drenched Honest John Daley.

"My man can't . . . I won't let him . . ."

Burgess was in tears, Buchanan realized. The tough man cradled Ford's head in his arms and rocked, moaning. Ford was unconscious but still trying weakly to rise.

Buchanan went to them, Coco at his side. Holley proffered the dry towels. Among them they picked up the fallen fighter and carried him to the corner. The duke was there with brandy. They applied the smelling salts.

Ford opened his eyes, drank the liquor. "What round is it? How am I doin'?"

Burgess said in a surprisingly clear, small voice, "Ya met a better man, Dan."

Coco put his arm around Ford. "I never met a better."

The duke said, "I say, shouldn't we get the ladies to shelter?"

The rain had not relented. The arena was already all but empty. They huddled together, going up the aisle, out to the office where Charlie Emory was supposed to be waiting with the money to pay off the fighters.

Buchanan stumbled over a prone figure. Wiping his eyes he saw that it was an armed man. A guard, he knew at once. His right hand went to his belt buckle. He held the deringer ready as he warned the others back. He stalked the door of the jerry-built office.

It was off the hinges. He stepped inside. One glance told the story. Charlie Emory's bald head was staved in, his blood staining the wooden floor. A safe gaped open.

Buchanan felt for a pulse, found none. The little promoter had died on the doorstep of his greatest promotion.

Coco said, "And the money gone. The Cutlers."

"And where is Mme. Velvet?" asked Caroline. She stood on the threshold, one hand to her face, still totally in control of herself.

As if in reply Mme. Velvet's floor manager came running. "Buchanan! Buchanan! Got to talk to you."

Buchanan said, "What happened?"

"She never came down. She was gone when I went to wake her up this morning. And she didn't come down through the place, neither. There's always someone to watch."

"The Cutlers," said Coco.

"Get the police, someone," said Buchanan. "And Coco, we better get on a train."

"A train?"

"If what I read in those papers and what I got a big hunch about is true . . . we get on the train for Boulder."

The duke said, "Oh, I say. In the mountains?"

"You follow me real good," said Buchanan.

They started from the arena. Burgess howled, "The money! The purse! They stole the damn purse."

"There's money downtown somewhere," Buchanan told him. "Advance sale. You take care of it."

Burgess said, "You damn right I'll take care of it. And if I never see the goddam West again it'll be too soon."

Buchanan watched him leave with Ford, still dazed, leaning on his shoulder. "Didn't take him long to get back to bein' himself."

"I think we'd better hurry," said the duke.

"We? This is no part of your concern."

"The Cutler cousins are my concern," said the duke. "We go."

And so they went in the driving rain.

* * *

The train rumbled toward Boulder, filled with
early departures from the big fight, everyone soaked
to the skin. They had piled Mme. Velvet's hair under
a shapeless hat and clad her in a stolen cloak, and
they thought it very funny that they had bought a
half-fare ticket for Cal Cutler's "son." She was seething with anger and also sick with fear. She had seen
them kill the one guard who had not sought shelter
from the storm.

Cal Cutler was saying, "Y' see, Providence is on
our side. All those preparations for decoyin' the
guards and the rain took care of it. And us. Hated t'
kill that one. We came a long way without killin'. It
was Buchanan started it to happen up in Cheyenne."

Chris Cutler said, "You go on about Buchanan,
you really do. We got what we need. We can skedad-
dle out of Colorado and they'll never find us."

"No one knows us for true. Only . . ." Con Cutler
nodded at Mme. Velvet. She shivered under their
regard.

Cal Cutler said, "By the time she gets loose, if she
does, we'll be long gone."

It did not reassure her. They looked so young and
innocent and happy that no one suspected nor would
suspect them, yet she felt the coldness, the rigid
determination in them. They had offered her no
indignity, they had only threatened her with the
black men.

They had learned of the victory of Coco over Ford
from the passengers. It did not set well with them.
They talked of "the damn nigger" and how all the
niggers would be uppity now and would have to be
put down. They bragged that Toby and Stonewall
would never take on airs because they were "the
right kind of nigras." It was apparent that "good
blacks" were "nigras" and all others "niggers."

It was a slow trip because of the blinding storm. When they arrived in Boulder they split up. Cal Cutler took charge of Mme. Velvet, ushering her out into the rain and to the side of the tracks where Toby and Stonewall had horses ready. They put her up with Cal Cutler and she was hideously uncomfortable on the ride up the road to the mountains.

They climbed and climbed. At last they made a sharp turn and came to the mouth of the deserted mine. It still rained and nearby Boulder Creek roared.

Cal Cutler said, "We can make a fire but you don't have a change of clothes. So you better just wrap in a blanket while we dry what you got on."

She did not reply. She went deep into the black hole and took off her clothing and threw it out to them. She accepted a soiled, smelly blanket, wiping herself as best she could. She could see the black men hanging her garments near a fire. No one came near her. They were a peculiar lot, she thought. Rape was not in their minds. They must have a code of their own, she thought. Maybe they did regret killing the guard. Maybe Buchanan had become a symbol of bad luck because his presence in their neighborhood had made them kill.

Cal Cutler was talking again. "When we get some food in us and collect everything and split it up we'll go around that winding road we found and ride out. The rain'll cover our tracks. Like I say, the good Lord is on our side."

One of the others said, "Maybe we should ride out now, eat on the road. You goin' to take her?"

"She's with us until we know we're safe," said Cal Cutler. "She could save us if they caught up with us."

"I know what you mean. Then we won't have to kill her."

"Not unless."

She wrapped the blanket tighter.

"Unless they do keep comin'?"

"That's right."

"She's real pretty."

"I noted that," said Cal Cutler.

"I dunno," said Chris Cutler. "She ain't a lady, y'know."

"She always behaved like one," said Cal Cutler. "You mind your upbringin', Chris. What we been doin' we been robbin' Yankees to pay for what they did to us. We were raised by God-fearin' people and we're goin' back and start again. That's why we're here."

Chris said, "But you want to fight Buchanan. You talked and talked about it."

"I can give that up. I can give up anything to get us back what's rightly ours. Youall better believe me."

"We do, Cal, we do," they chorused.

He had them under control, she thought. He was as big as Buchanan in this setting. He was drying his shirt and she could see the muscles bulging down his spine. He was a strange man and as dangerous as a grizzly. She hunkered down and waited for her clothing.

Cal Cutler brought her clothing, also a tin plate of cold meat and stale bread. He said, "Give me the blanket." He blocked the view of the others.

"Peeping Toms?" she asked. "My, you are a gent."

"In the South we are taught to treat a lady like a whore and a whore like a lady," he said.

"Good old South," she said. "Wonderful land of mammy and yams and people like you."

She donned her wrinkled, damp clothing.

He said, "People like us will restore the country. If you behave and if all goes well you may live to see it."

"Sufficient unto the day." She was afraid but she had to reply. Their arrogance offended her to the depths. "I heard you talk about Buchanan. The day I'd like to see is when you do get to fight him."

The contempt in her voice stung him. He flung down the blanket and said, "Woman, if we do have to kill you . . ." He broke off. "Do not press me, ma'am. Eat and be ready to ride."

He strode back to the fire. There was a tremendous clap of thunder. The storm, which had begun here in the mountains, struck with force that shook the earth. At the entrance to the mine the black men cried out.

She followed as they all ran. Water roared, wave upon wave. It was a flash flood of huge proportions. In a moment it had engulfed Boulder Creek and turned it into a raging sea cascading down the hills.

They were cut off. They stood like statues, knowing it. She felt exultation, immediately followed by knowledge of increased danger.

Cal Cutler said, "They haven't found us. Break out the boxes of shells. Look to your guns. We still have the woman."

That was it. They still had her. She went back into the mine tunnel, made a cushion of the blanket and settled herself.

In the hotel Buchanan had changed into dry clothing and was filling a bandolier with bullets. He strapped on two revolvers and filled his belt. Coco watched, shaking his head.

"Guns. It always comes to it. Guns."

"You saw the dead men," Buchanan said sharply. "You know they'll kill. You know they must have grabbed Mme. Velvet."

"It ain't that I say you shouldn't. I just wish nobody did."

Buchanan said, "We lost Reiner. The crowd, I never did see such a crowd."

"I thought the train would never get here."

"Drunk people, happy people, sad people. People. People. And the Cutlers."

Coco said, "They're up yonder."

"Yes. That we know. They were seen this time. Dumb luck that anyone was left to see 'em."

It had been the telegraph operator, stuck at his post, who had caught a glimpse of them riding out, who had reported that a small boy was with them. The small boy had to be Mme. Velvet, Buchanan knew. They were smart right up to the finish, they knew enough to take a hostage. They left nothing to chance.

He said, "Good. Go down and ask them to put up some food. It may be a long chase."

"In this-here storm?"

"We don't know about the storm. We can't figure on it."

Coco said, "I'm goin'."

As he went out the door Lady Caroline appeared. "May I come in?"

He closed the door behind her and they kissed as naturally as though they were a married couple. She was wearing men's garments and storm boots. She pulled away and said, "Without Bob Reiner we can't rouse the men. They take orders from him, do they not, now?"

"He'll be here sooner or later. Coco and I will ride ahead. You come with Reiner."

She shook her head. "Bertie won't hear of it, y'know."

"Why should you people ride out in this weather lookin' for trouble? There'll be shootin' if we find them."

"Bertie never quit anything. We're a group that does things together."

"Bertie never quit anything. We're a group that does things together."

"But this is loco."

"Loco weed. Maybe it also grows in England." She laughed. "Not only is he going along, Bertie's bringing his camera. Just in case, he says."

"I never heard of the British bein' loco. Maybe the weed does grow over there. It plain don't make sense."

"Bertie never claimed to make sense. Perhaps that's why we all love him so?"

"You could lose him in the mountains," Buchanan said. "Any of us could be lost. The storm alone is dangerous enough."

"We shan't walk by Boulder Creek again, now, shall we?"

"No, ma'am. We'll be lucky if we can ride." He knew it would be bootless to try to change their minds. They were what they were, undaunted, brave, simple folk. Their kind, he thought, had settled the country right in the beginning. Maybe they were foolish, rash, but they had courage over and beyond the ordinary. He shouldered his saddlebags. "Time's a-wastin', Caroline."

She rose on tiptoe to kiss his cheek. "Oh, Tom, I do wish you'd come to England with us. It would be so . . . right."

"Reckon you people are too crazy for me." He grinned at her.

They were in the bar, all dressed for the storm. He made one more try. "Bertie, this ain't right. This is no part of your business. The ladies, don't you see what can happen up yonder?"

Bertie said, "Begged them to stay here, y'know. Always been like that, since they were little girls."

"It's my fight. I'd rather make it alone."

"Do have a touch." The duke poured from his

private bottle. "Bringing a bit of this along. Good in rainy weather."

"This ain't exactly rainy weather. This is a mountain storm. It's dangerous just to ride into the mountains. You never saw a flash flood."

"Maybe I could photograph one." Bertie smiled. His blue eyes were guileless. "This is adventure, y'know. I came here never expectin' this kind of a game."

There was no way to prevent them. Buchanan led them to the livery stable. Coco had brought food to be distributed amongst them. The horses were ready. Buchanan checked the gear, the arms. The duke and Brister both had American rifles. The duchess was sporting a light hunting gun. Caroline had a shotgun. He took it from her.

"If you fired this it would break your shoulder," he told her. "Let's hope you don't need a weapon."

"Oh, I have this." She produced a small pearl-handled .32 Smith & Wesson. "Bob gave it to me."

"Fine," said Buchanan. Reiner was a damned fool, he thought. Such a gun had no place in the West. The man was head over heels in love with her.

He hoped Reiner got back to Boulder in time to roust out the posse which might well be needed. Three Cutler cousins and two black men could stand off an army if they were anywhere near where he believed them to be.

He ran over in his mind the terrain he had scouted. The others mounted up. Nightshade was skittery, as always after a spell in the stable. He talked the black horse down, not wanting to battle him through a bucking scene. The mountain camp had been on the east of Boulder Creek. Therefore he figured the Cutlers would be above and as high as they could safely climb. They would want high gun and seclusion.

There was a chance they had got away, storm or no storm. If they moved fast, with the start their early departure from Denver had given them they could be gone. Picking up track in the rain would be impossible. It seemed to him that the great storm had been designed to help the Cutlers on their way.

They rode up the wet, slippery trail, as motley a crew as Buchanan had ever seen. He and Coco led, then came the women, with the duke and Brister in the middle. And Brister carried the camera, unwieldy as it was.

Coco said, "Night's gonna fall on us afore we get anywhere."

"The cabins," Buchanan told him. "Just in case."

The road was knee deep in water. They struggled up the slope until they could see ahead the outlines of the fight camp. Buchanan let them pass him, listening to Boulder Creek. When they were safely indoors he pointed Nightshade toward the roar of the stream.

In a moment he knew what had happened. He could not see above. The darkness and the heavy sheet of rain limited his vision to a hundred yards or so. But he knew. There had been a flash flood and the Cutlers could well be trapped.

He had thought that the storm was on the other side. He glanced upward, taking rain in his face and eyes and said, "So maybe that's the way it's supposed to be. I ain't got much religion but I got a little faith."

He rode back to the cabins. Brister was bustling about in the largest, the only one still furnished. There were blankets and kindling and wood for the stove. The food which Coco had provided was scanty but enough.

Caroline asked, "Coco, aren't you worn out?"

"No, ma'am."

"But you had a terrific fight."

"Yes, ma'am. He was a good one."

"And you're not tired?"

"Oh, I'm tired, ma'am. But tired ain't worn out."

"We trained," said the duke. "Nothin' like it, y' know."

Brister served wine. There was always wine, somehow or other. Wine and good whiskey. These were the best people Buchanan had ever roughed it with. He told them as much.

The duke said, "Good show," and raised his glass.

They drank and Buchanan said, "Better sleep. Tomorrow will be rougher'n today."

He and Coco took off in the rain. They went into the cabin they had occupied during the training. The bunks were not made up but there were blankets folded in a cupboard. They had traveled light, without their bedrolls, but both had slept on harder surfaces.

Buchanan thought of the fight, of the robbery and of the British girl. Then he slept.

It was the silence which roused him. It was still dark and Boulder Creek still ran full but the sound had lessened to a large degree. He padded to the door.

The storm had stopped abruptly. There was a moon floating free of the vanishing clouds. He wakened Coco.

"Let's get goin'," he said.

"What about the others?"

"We can't let them come up into the mountains and face the damn Cutlers. Never intended to. Just be quiet."

"They ain't goin' to like it."

"Uh-huh," said Buchanan. "The horses."

They went very quietly about the business of saddling up. They set their path through mud borne down by the floods, and headed toward the camp of the Cutlers which Buchanan had found earlier.

The going was difficult. Mud and rocks were strewn as if a giant had been playing childish games. The moon alone was friendly, lighting their way. Buchanan sat Nightshade at the campsite and reasoned it out.

"There's only one way they'd go. That's up. I had a reckoning on possibles last time I was here."

Coco said, "Higher up is mighty high."

"That's where I'd be." He was putting himself in the place of the Cutlers. "Then I'd try to sneak around the top and go down the other side. Movin' fast, it could be done."

"But they can't get out tonight."

"It's mornin' and they're flooded in for maybe an hour or two, maybe more. The runoff'll be swift but not that quick."

Coco asked, "How we goin' to get the lady away from 'em?"

"Haven't figured that one out. Haven't figured how we can handle five jaspers like them."

"You better had," said Coco. "One way or 'tother."

They started the ride. The horses slipped and slid. Water sloshed around them. Boulder Creek seemed not to slacken although they knew it did as it cascaded downward.

It was the Cutler fire that gave them away. They had not allowed it to go out because of the dampness, fearing for their ammunition as well as their comfort. Buchanan spotted a wisp of smoke. The operating mines were silent, not working in the storm—and owing to the big fight in Denver, which had drawn away the workers.

"That's it," he said. "We'll leave the horses. Keep low and . . . well, you been on the scout before."

"Never did like it," said Coco.

They left Nightshade and the chestnut in a gully

where the water had drained off. Buchanan took his
rifle and strapped on the bandolier. It was bulky and
uncomfortable but he had every reason to believe he
would need it.

They began the long and difficult crawl up the
soaked slope of the mountain. If it were possible to
get behind them, Buchanan thought, they might be
surprised. On the other hand, no one could predict
how they would respond. And . . . there was Mme.
Velvet.

Mme. Velvet sat on a flat rock and listened to Cal
Cutler. The cessation of the storm had diminished
her hopes. She had slept badly and very little and
the meager fire could not truly warm her.

Cal Cutler said, "It's goin' down fast. We got that
flat space right below us. If we can get around this
hilltop and go on west, then north, we'll be clear.
The storm helped us and the storm is goin' to set us
free."

"It's always worked out," said Chris.

"The good Lord's on our side, all right," said Con.

The black men said nothing. They were busy
gathering parcels of money and jewels and putting
them into sacks to be carried by them. Madame
Velvet's eyes widened at the enormous amount of
loot. She had a good mind for figures and calculated
there was more in those sacks than she handled in a
year.

Cal Cutler was looking at her. "Maybe you'd like
to come along with us and open a house in Alabama."

"No, thanks," she said. "There's too much blood in
those sacks."

"Not our fault," he shouted. "That damn Buchanan. Your friend. He's the one started the killin'."

"The James Boys had friends until they started

137

killing," she said. "I mind when they holed up in Texas nobody would tell on 'em."

"We beat the James gang," Cal Cutler said. "They never got as much as we have. I said we'd beat 'em and we did."

"They ain't caught yet," she said. "And neither are you. But it hasn't ended yet, has it?"

"We'll see about that, ma'am." He quieted down, confident. "Nobody's goin to take us. Nobody."

"And you won't get to fight Buchanan."

"That I do regret." He grinned at her. "I'd like for you and all his friends to see that."

"Like I said, I'd give a country farm to see it." She lapsed into silence as he described what he would do to Buchanan had he the chance. He posed, he made motions with his fists, he strutted. The man's ego was overwhelming. She silently wondered if he would have a chance in such a meeting.

Chris said, "You'd beat him, Cal. But better we should hightail it outa here."

"Not yet. The damn creek is still too strong. Can't risk losin' a horse in a flood."

Con Cutler said, "Can't risk a posse comin', neither."

"Even then. We got the woman."

"Yeah. We got the woman."

They all looked at her as if she were part of their loot. She stared back at them, trying desperately not to show that she was afraid.

The duke said, "Caroline, my dear sister, you should know that Buchanan would not allow us to put ourselves in danger."

"I know."

"Then please calm yourself, m' dear."

"He's up there against that crew of killers and I'm not with him."

"You feel that strongly?"

138

"I do."

"But you know that it is impossible." His voice was kindly.

"Nothing is impossible."

"He would never leave his beloved country, now, would he?"

"I could remain here."

He smiled. "Darlin', you could not. The man is a free soul. A hunter, not a homemaker."

"But such a man, brother."

"You may not meet his like again. So take what you can have. Love him, but know the end."

"I refuse!"

"Ah, well. Love makes the world go 'round and all that. But we are realists, are we not? Think."

She turned and walked away. The sun was shining and riders were coming in. She recognized Bob Reiner. Behind him were Alex, Tony and Dax and several other armed men. She waited.

Reiner said, "I got here as soon as I could. Where is Buchanan?"

She pointed upward. "He left before we were awake."

"Did he leave any word?"

"No. He did not want us to be with him."

"Of course not." He scowled. "I'm no tracker. But I know these mountains. I'll take a chance. And I'll spread the men. The miners know all the deserted diggings. Will you be all right?"

"No." She laughed. "Not here."

"You can't go up there."

She gave him a direct look. "Where Buchanan is, there I mean to be. I saw dead men, killed by the Cutlers."

"It's not your affair, Caroline. Leave it to me."

"I make it my affair." She became regal. "We shall be there. You may depend upon it." She turned and ran into the cabin.

Reiner swallowed hard. He sat a moment, looking after her. Then he gave orders to the miners.

Indoors Caroline was highly excited. "We have guides. We can at least follow and try to join Buchanan and Coco."

"Of course, m' dear," said Bertie. "Are you up to it, darlin'?"

His wife said, "I wouldn't miss it, dear."

"The camera, Brister?"

"Yes, sir."

"What a chance for great pictures! Imagine, a fight to the death. And now the sun. What luck!"

They all were satisfied that good fortune was with them. They moved quickly, getting to the horses. Reiner watched them. The posse was already weaving through the hills with care, upward toward the peaks, well knowing the terrain.

Caroline said, "Lead on, Macduff, and damned be he who cries enough."

"I wish you wouldn't," said Reiner.

"Your wish is not my command." She was in high spirits, kindly but determined.

He recognized defeat. "Then keep close to me. My men will do the scouting. When we find them, please do as I say."

Brister carried the camera. They rode with Reiner.

Buchanan was looking for a vantage from which to dicker. He was sure they had Mme. Velvet. The mountains were far from bare, there were trees, there was foliage and there was too much water.

Coco said, "Seems like there's too much ground to cover."

There was a narrow trickle coming down the mountain. Buchanan said, "Only bare ground is in front of that damn mine."

"They can't get away without us seein' 'em."

"That's the only good part of it." He stepped over the water onto a flat rock.

The rock slid. He went down, all two hundred and forty pounds of him. He put out his left hand and felt a shock of pain. He sat cursing himself for a fool, for taking his eyes off the footing to watch the entrance of the Cutler retreat. The ache did not go away. He opened and closed his fist and gingerly swung the arm. He was well accustomed to injury. He thought nothing was broken but he had a bad sprain. His left wrist was swelling.

Coco helped him to his feet. They were in a copse of heavy fir trees.

Buchanan said, "It's okay. We circle around. Look for a spot."

"You done hurt that arm. You had a bullet in that arm one time."

"Uh-huh. I also had an arrow in it once. Didn't kill me." But it continued to hurt.

The sun began to do its work. Steam rose from their wet clothing. Buchanan paused, his eye on the mouth of the Cutler stronghold. They were making preparations but the overflow from Boulder Creek still blocked their progress to any direction excepting eastward or northward, either of which would bring them toward the town and into trouble.

Now the steam made little eddies across the landscape. Buchanan and Coco ducked low and ran, concealed by the mist. They came to a sturdy clump of live oak near the creek. They stayed low, squatting, watching.

Buchanan said in a whisper, "Sound carries up here. You see what's happenin'?"

"They want to go and they can't."

"You catch sight of Mme. Velvet?"

"We don't even know they got her."

"You want to bet on it?"

"Oh, no. I just wanta see her."

"We'll find out soon enough."

"You ain't goin' to make one of those fool runs at 'em, are you, Tom? They're bad people."

"I'd be a sittin' duck. No, we got to sorta surprise 'em."

"How we do that? They got eyes comin' this way."

"There's got to be a way."

"You figure on it."

"Uh-huh." But he could think of nothing brilliant. Their position was too strong. If he could come down from behind—but that was impossible because of the water and because of the time element. He took his eyes off the mine entrance long enough to survey the scene.

The creek had subsided to a degree. There were two boulders, brought down by the flood, which were twenty feet from the bank. They were on higher ground. Between them there was a space bare of all but low, tough shrubs.

He said, "Coco, you stay right here."

"Where you goin'?"

"Right over yonder."

He took a deep breath. His left side hurt. The rifle seemed clumsy. Still, it was a good spot. He ran.

The shrubs and the rising steam helped. He slipped and almost fell again, recovered himself. He lunged the last few paces. He curled up and measured his position.

He was not quite level with the mine entry but he could command a view of all that went on. The big rock gave fair protection. He would be subject to a stray ricochet but that was a chance he could take.

He resumed his attention to the Cutlers. They were seeing to their saddles and gear. The water was running off the flat area and down the hills. They would be ready to depart in a very short time.

He wondered when was the best time to brace them. It would have to be sudden, dramatic, stunning, or they would kill him out of hand.

Actually, he thought, he didn't have a chance. They were too many. He could cut down a couple, maybe three. Then the Cutlers would take shelter and fight it out.

Cal Cutler beckoned. One of the blacks led out a tiny figure. It was Mme. Velvet.

Now the fat was surely in the fire. He had really known it. A part of his brain had tried to reject it but there it had been all the while. If he fired now they would certainly do away with her. That would be their first thought . . . or would it?

Would they instead parley for their lives? Would they accept a loss and make a deal? He doubted it. They were not of that cunning stripe. They were men with a cause, however misguided it might be.

Valuable time was passing. It occurred to him that he had been thinking of the unthinkable. He had never fired on anyone without first giving a warning. He had suffered some wounds from this peculiarity of his. The frontier life did not admit of giving quarter when criminals, killers were involved. It was Buchanan's own credo which deterred him.

He could wait no longer. He called out in his most stentorian voice, "Hold on, there. Don't try to move out."

They whirled around as one, their rifles ready. They scanned the scene, muzzles of the guns training on every possible hiding place.

Buchanan called, "Right here behind the rocks. If you shoot be sure you're right."

Two Cutlers swung guns his way. Cal Cutler threw up a hand. They lowered the rifles.

He said, "Buchanan."

"That's the name."

"You might take note, we got the woman."

"I see her."

Cal Cutler motioned to one of the blacks, who dutifully presented a gun to the head of Mme. Velvet.

"You know how it is, then. We'd shuck her like an ear of corn if you come down on us."

"Uh-huh. And then I'd give 'em the word and they'd cut youall down like sheaves of wheat."

"You got no people out there. Nobody but you could run up on us like this."

"You sure of that?"

"I'm mighty sure. We're goin' out, Buchanan. One man can't stop us. There purely ain't a way."

"You say."

"You fire a shot and we kill the woman."

"Could be. But how many of you will be left?"

"One man is enough. We're goin' home, Buchanan. You don't know what that means."

"I don't give a damn," Buchanan told him. "Might be nary one of you will go anywheres."

"This is a waste of talk and time," said Cal Cutler. "We're movin'."

The voice of Bob Reiner called, "If you do you're deader than Adam. All of you."

Cal Cutler whirled around. For a long moment he stared. Buchanan held his breath. His bluff had turned out to be an ace in the hole. Somehow Reiner had found them and it was certain that he had not come alone.

"You believe me now, Cutler?" he called.

"There's still the woman."

"You kill her and I'll see you don't die here. I'll see you hanged. Choked to death, Cutler. You want to end at the gallows?"

"The woman dies first." He leaned his rifle against the mountainside and pulled his revolver. He pointed it at the middle of Mme. Velvet's body. "I swear I'll gut-shoot her. You know what kind of death that is, Buchanan."

Reiner called again. "Say the word, Buchanan. We'll cut them all down."

"She'll still die," said Cal Cutler. There was no doubt in the minds of any of them that he was telling the truth. He was fanatic. The black men stood like statues, under perfect control. All were ready to be martyred for their belief.

"It's a damn fool way to go," Buchanan said.

"If I know you Yankees, you won't let it happen. You give us your word that we can ride out and she'll live."

"No bargaining," Buchanan told him. He saw Mme. Velvet as she turned pale. He hastily added, "Unless you got a better idea."

Reiner said, "There's no way out, Cutler. You're completely surrounded. Best surrender."

"Lee surrendered. Then came the deluge," Cutler cried.

"Think it over," Buchanan suggested. "Think it all the way through. See where you stand, where that trip down South back home stands right now."

There was a long silence. Men moved along the slope of the mountain. Cal Cutler was sunk in deep thought, the muzzle of his revolver still against Mme. Velvet's middle.

She suddenly spoke. "You think you can beat him. Why don't you fight Buchanan for the game?"

Cal Cutler laughed on a harsh note. "You think he'd take that up? He'd rather see you dead just so he can get us all."

Coco called out, "Don't do it, Tom."

It was the arm, of course. Buchanan looked down at his wrist, which was red and puffed. Coco was warning him. Cal Cutler poised, waiting, then he spoke.

"There's your deal, Buchanan. I'll fight you. Eve'body thinks you're cock o' the walk. I'll meet you man to man for the whole matter. I win, we take the lady for safety sake and go. I promise to turn her loose if we get free. You win, and you get it all."

Reiner yelled, "No, Buchanan. We've got 'em dead to rights. Don't do it."

"He's right, Tom," said Coco. "Don't you do it. They can't get away nohow."

Buchanan was watching Mme. Velvet. She was very small and very lost. Her life dangled on a thread. He remembered how gay she had been and how straightforward. His kind of woman, he had thought, if it were not for Lady Caroline.

Cal Cutler said, "I knew he wouldn't do it. He's a gunman, not a fighter."

"Don't, please." It was the voice of Caroline. "You know he's a killer. They'll shoot you in the back."

They would not, Buchanan thought. Not while they held the lady. There was this weirdness about them. If Cal Cutler made a deal they would stand by it, he felt. It was not that he feared assassination. It was the pain in his wrist and shoulder. Cal Cutler was a big man. He must have a reason, Buchanan thought, to believe he can whip me. He must be good with his hands. He doesn't know I'm handicapped. Therefore he has to be a fighter, a good one. A boxer, perhaps, like the duke, an amateur but a big, strong one. All this ran through his mind even as he put down his rifle and began to take off his bandolier, then his revolvers and cartridge belt. He tried his left arm. It was stiff and sore. He would not have full use of it, he knew. The old wounds were acting up because of his stupid fall. It came down to Mme. Velvet.

They had been shrewd. They had coppered their

bets. Given a small amount of time they would have got clean away, taking her with them. If no posse caught up with them she might have had a chance. If one did, they would kill her without compunction.

They were smart, all right. He removed the wide belt with the deringer in the buckle. Cal Cutler knew about it; Buchanan could not risk bringing danger on them all by keeping it on him. He knew everyone would be crowding in for the fight. He could see it all, he was measuring distances, the condition of the wet, flat surface on which they would meet.

At last he arose from behind the rocks. There was a moment when it seemed Cutler or one of his cohorts would shoot. Reiner shouted and that danger passed. Buchanan went forward in his soft boots.

Coco popped out of hiding like a jack-in-the-box. At the mine entrance guns came up. Cal Cutler struck them down.

Coco said, "You goin' to fight that big dude with one arm? Can you close that fist?"

Buchanan tried. "Nope."

"You plumb crazy, Tom."

"I made the deal."

"Lemme fight him with one hand."

"He don't want you. He wants me."

"It ain't right. Look on him."

Cal Cutler was removing his shirt. He had the perfect athlete's build. He was a handsome specimen, blond, wide shoulders, tapered waist, long, strong legs. He moved easily, like a puma on the prowl.

"Looks fine," said Buchanan. "Your turn to handle the corner. Won't be any rules, though."

Coco said, "He'll beat on you, Tom."

"Dan Ford beat on you."

"Different game," Coco insisted. "This is a mistake."

"Could be." Buchanan removed his shirt. The scars of many battles were noticeable but there was no fat on him. The training had trimmed him down under his normal weight. He felt light and strong except for the injury.

Now the others came to the scene. Brister had the camera and was setting it up. The duke joined Coco and Buchanan. His wife and Lady Caroline were not far behind, nor was Bob Reiner. It was he who first discovered the swollen left wrist.

"Buchanan, is this sensible? You're hurt."

"The world goes on," Buchanan said. "You plays the cards they deal you."

Cal Cutler paused in the middle of the cleared space. It was still wet. He looked at the oncoming group of armed men. He said, "No tricks. We'll shoot if there's a trick."

"No tricks," said Buchanan. "You shoot and we're all dead."

"I've wanted this since I met you."

"In Cheyenne," said Buchanan.

"I'm the man you can't beat."

"Uh-huh," said Buchanan. "Want to get on with it?"

"Nothing barred."

"You want it that way it's okay with me."

"I'm takin' your word on this."

"You got a choice?"

"That's no never mind. Your word, they tell me, is good."

Buchanan said, "Uh-huh." He was hiding his left arm as best he could. He was thinking about defense and attack.

Coco said, "I'll fight you with one hand tied behind my back."

"I don't fight with niggers," said Cal Cutler. "If you're ready, Buchanan."

"Ready."

The duke had maneuvered his camera to take in the entire scene, including the Cutlers and the blacks at the mine entrance. Brister was standing with him. The women had moved to the front rank of spectators. Caroline was clenching her fists.

Coco said, "All right . . . time!"

Cutler moved with creditable speed. He lunged forward with a swift left jab. Buchanan ducked and countered with a right which was partially blocked. Cutler danced, showing some skill. Buchanan pivoted, not following, waiting. He held his left hand high. It was of little use but he warded off the next attack, accepting the pain in his forearm, holding back his right fist.

He knew about defense from Coco; always block or ward off with the left, counter with the right. Cutler came in strong, and hammer blows struck Buchanan's left arm. It dropped.

Cutler threw a hard right. It stung and Buchanan slipped in the slick mud and went down.

Cutler was on him, kicking hard with a pointed boot. He caught Buchanan in the ribs, again on the left side.

Caroline cried, "Oh, shame!"

Coco warned her, "Nothin' barred."

Up at the mine Mme. Velvet covered her face. Tears flowed for the first time since she had been captured. The Cutlers and the blacks were cheering.

Buchanan rolled. He caught Cutler's heel on the next kick. Using his right hand he applied pressure. Cutler's ankle twisted, he lost balance and went down. Buchanan was quickly on his feet.

"The boots!" The yell came from the miners. "Give 'im the bloody boots!"

Buchanan stepped back. He let Cutler get to his knees. Then he swung an uppercut from his heels. Cutler went sailing back, skidding, rolling, floundering. Buchanan followed him. He was tempted but he could not use the boot.

Cutler reached out with great speed, grabbing Buchanan's knees. They came together with a thump. They gouged and punched to little avail, too close to do damage.

The crowd was howling, drowning out the Cutler voices. Mme. Velvet dared to look again. Powder flashed. The duke had taken a picture of the entire scene. The Cutlers flinched, almost began to shoot, then realized what had happened. What they did not realize was that they were forever imprinted on wet-plate for the world to recognize.

Buchanan got his right hand on Cutler's shoulder and heaved him away. He got to one knee. His left arm hung limply at his side. Cutler's eyes widened, then narrowed. He charged.

Buchanan threw him over his shoulder. Cutler landed on his feet and came back swinging, circling to Buchanan's left. Buchanan came around, defending himself against a furious attack.

Coco called, "Lefty, Tom, lefty."

It was the only thing to do. He presented his right side to Cutler. He hammered short blows to the chest. Cutler gave ground under thunderous punches. Buchanan swung another right but Cutler slipped again to Buchanan's left. He landed a blow to the face and blood ran from a cut on Buchanan's cheek.

Caroline said, "Oh, no. This is not sporting, Bertie."

"Chances of the game." He was lining up another shot, aiming to get the Cutler gang in the background.

The duchess took Caroline's hand and said, "Don't look."

"I . . . I have to look. He may be killed. The man will kick him to death, given the chance."

They were at it again. Mme. Velvet was going with the punches now, her small body swaying. Her eyes were like stars as she whispered, "One punch, Buchanan, one punch."

"One punch," mocked Chris Cutler. "He'll never land it."

It seemed true. Cutler, fast afoot, skidding in the mud but maintaining balance, walked around Buchanan, always keeping to his right. Buchanan pivoted, unwilling to attack with one able hand, watching a chance for counter-punch. He had felt the strength of Cutler and knew his chances were slim. He was a bit dizzy from the increasing pain in his arm and shoulder.

Cutler dove in, a surprising move, butting. Buchanan brought up his knee and struck downward with his right. Cutler went headfirst into a puddle and skidded. Again Buchanan waited for him to get up.

Reiner said to the duke, "Look up there. We could blast them away with one volley without hitting the woman."

Bertie said, "And could we live with ourselves?"

"It would be murder," said the duchess.

Reiner bit his tongue. He jittered, watching Buchanan struggle against the strong young outlaw. Cutler was giving two punches for every one he received. He was blocking most of Buchanan's predictable rights, always dancing to the weak side. Buchanan was bleeding from the nose.

Coco called again. "Get in close, Tom. Work downstairs."

Buchanan tried to obey. He came in, took two jabs, dug for the body. Cutler's rib cage was hard with muscle. The two men slugged it out, Cutler with both hands, Buchanan with one.

151

It was an uneven struggle, Mme. Velvet knew. She wondered if she should try to grab a gun and shoot it out with the gang. They were paying no attention to her, their attention fixed on the fight. Then she realized that she would die in the attempt.

Buchanan was standing like a bull in a pasture as Cutler ran around him. The footing was becoming firmer by the minute. Buchanan felt strong despite the pain. His target was elusive, he had to suffer to inflict a light blow. Cutler was like quicksilver, in and out, darting punches to the head and to the sore left side.

Buchanan saw an opening for a left. He switched and landed a right to the body. Cutler drew a deep breath, tin-canning, boxing. Buchanan followed. Cutler sidestepped and landed another blow to the face. Buchanan's left eye began to swell. A few more blows and he would lose the sight in it, he knew.

Again Cutler came in and tried to wrestle, confident in his strength against a crippled Buchanan. He grabbed for the left arm. Buchanan took it away with an effort and leaned his shoulder into Cutler's chest. Again his right went to the body.

He felt Cutler give. No human could endure Buchanan's powerful body punches.

He charged and Cutler used speed to evade him, stuck out a foot. Buchanan tripped and fell. Cutler dashed in to administer a coup de grâce with a hard kick to the head.

Buchanan felt the breeze as he pulled his head away. He swung a long leg. He caught Cutler behind the knees. Cutler went down in a heap, his legs doubling under him.

Buchanan arose. He wiped blood from his face. He heard the miners' cry, "Finish 'im, Buchanan, finish 'im."

He waited, crouching a little. Cutler got up slowly. Now he was not so swift, limping. Buchanan went in close. Cutler fought like a tiger, slamming both hands to head and body. Buchanan punched short and hard.

They stood and traded, two big, strong men, one with two hands, the other with but one.

It was Cutler who retreated. Buchanan hit him with a right to the nose. Cutler stumbled, gore running down to his mouth, where he could taste the saltiness. He instinctively raised a hand to wipe it away.

Buchanan hit him again. This time it was to the body. Cutler doubled over and turned away. Buchanan moved in.

Cutler kicked hard for the groin. Buchanan, too late to retreat, turned his leg and caught it on the thigh. Now there was pain throughout his body.

"I say," said the duke. "This is a bit much, isn't it?"

"He'll be killed," sobbed Caroline. "I know he'll be killed. Can't we stop it?"

"Nonsense, dear," said Bertie.

Mme. Velvet was praying. She had not prayed in many a long year and the words did not come easily but she was trying. The Cutlers and the black men were jumping up and down and howling encouragement.

Reiner said, "I still think a bargain with murderers is not binding. I'd fire on them."

"And kill that lady? You know she'd die either under our fire or theirs," Bertie said sharply.

Caroline said, "It's not the way. Only a miracle can save Buchanan now."

Buchanan was standing stock-still. Cutler was still limping but seemed as strong as ever, coming in, boxing against a crippled opponent, picking his spots, delivering hard blows. Buchanan fended off as many as he could with his right hand. His left arm now hung useless at his side. Blood ran freely down his face. The sun was hot, the air was clear, his vision was good, but his weaponry seemed useless.

Cutler was grinning, his teeth showing. He danced in, dragging the sore leg, and tried a hard right hand. It was a punch that could end it, would have ended it against a lesser man.

Buchanan leaned into it. He took it upon his neck muscles. He brought up a right uppercut in response.

He caught Cutler coming in. The fist landed on the jaw. Cutler stood up very straight. He seemed ready to continue, took a step forward. Buchanan watched him.

Cutler fell on his face. He lay quite still. There was complete silence, then the mountainside rang with human sound.

Cutler rolled over once. He put a hand to earth. He slowly got to his knees. His nose was misshapen from the earlier blow. He staggered to his feet and doggedly started forward.

A murderer, thought Buchanan, a thief. Yet here was a courageous man. Here was one who did not quit, no matter the stage of the game.

Buchanan aimed his punch. He sent it from the side, a hook projected from the hip. He aimed it at the side of the jaw.

He felt the bone crack as it landed. Cutler went flying.

He landed on a shoulder and lay like a sack of wheat. He moved no more than a dead man. There was no question in the mind of anyone present. He would not rise again to fight that day.

The cousins on the hill let out a howl of despair. Mme. Velvet dashed down the hill toward the scene of the fight.

Chris Cutler raised a gun. At that moment the duke took his picture. Mme. Velvet was in line. Cutler's finger was on the trigger.

The flash blinded the gunman. His shot went wild.

It was a signal to those who had kept themselves in check. Reiner fired. The miners fired.

Chris Cutler fell. Con Cutler fell over him.

Mme. Velvet ran into the arms of Caroline. The two black men at the mine threw down their guns. The posse closed in upon them.

Buchanan stood silent amidst the turmoil. Coco was at his side, saying, "You got to be took care of. He hurt you bad."

"He hurt me." He was looking at the unconscious Cal Cutler. "Funny, ain't it? By fightin' me fair and square he saved himself for the gallows."

"How was he goin' to go any other way? Man lives like him, he's got to go down the path."

Buchanan said, "What a waste."

"He was game," Coco admitted. "But did you have two hands he would've gone quicker."

Reiner came to them. "They're not dead, the ones at the mine. How are you, Buchanan?"

"I seen better hours," Buchanan said. "Check the mine, check their gear. I think you'll find they're totin' a lot of what they stole."

"I'll do that."

Caroline and Mme. Velvet were coming toward him. Buchanan said to Coco, "I better get back to camp."

"You better get to a doctor."

"That too. Betwixt one thing and another I never been this busted up."

The women stopped, staring at him, at the blood, at his limp left arm. Their eyes were round with awe and sympathy.

He said, "We can talk later. Just get me on Nightshade."

Coco retrieved his shirt, draped it around his shoulders. They were having trouble bringing Cal

155

Cutler to consciousness. Buchanan walked to where he lay with miners working roughly on him.

He said, "Take it easy, men. He's got a lot to pay for. But today he don't need any more."

He went past them, stopped to speak to Bertie.

"You not only got a picture. You saved Madame's life with that flash. Everything has a place, my friend, everything has a time and a place."

He leaned a bit on Coco. They found the horses where they had left them. Buchanan crawled into the saddle. Nightshade whinnied as if he understood that his master was injured. Coco swung aboard the chestnut. They rode down the road toward Boulder.

The creek sang its song. It did not sound so merry to Buchanan. There were loose ends to be tied up and he was in no mood to think about them. For one of the few times in his life he was not hungry. He wanted only some medical aid and a night of sleep.

In the morning Buchanan moved experimentally, rolled out of bed. Coco was at his side in a second.

"You better not move too much, Tom."

He stretched his left arm, winced. Then he said, "Look. I can double up my fist."

"You ain't human."

He took a few steps. "My legs are fine."

"You got scars on your face. You got bruises on your belly. You oughta stay put for a time."

"What about the Cutlers?"

"They made a hospital outa the jail. The niggers are waitin' on em, mostly."

"You know they'll hang."

"Better men have stretched rope," said Coco.

"Uh-huh." Buchanan began to dress. The more he tried, the better he felt. His left arm was lame and sore but otherwise he felt no pain. The rigorous life stood him in good stead. "The duke?"

"Waitin' to see how you are this mornin'."

The loose Western clothing felt good on him. "I'm hungry."

"Lawsy, now I know you're okay. Down we go."

They went down into the lobby of the hotel. Everyone was there, including Mme. Velvet and Crocker, the cook, who ran up to Coco and wrung his hand.

"You won me enough to keep me in booze for a year. Praise be. Anything I can do, any old time, brother."

Coco said, "Just be good."

Crocker retreated. Caroline came and looked at Buchanan, a little crease between her eyes.

The duke said, "We'll be leaving for Denver on the next train. Have to pick up our winnin's first. Can't tell you how wonderful it's been."

Caroline said, "Can't you possibly go with us?"

Buchanan shook his head.

"I must go home, you know."

There was a bit of embarrassed silence. Bob Reiner moved uneasily, then sat down. The duke was impassive, as was his wife.

Buchanan said, "It's been . . . excitin', hasn't it?"

"Exciting," she agreed. For a long moment she waited.

Buchanan could not find words. He tried to smile and failed. It was clear to him now. It had been a romantic time, harmless if allowed to stay as it was, without further complications.

Caroline went on, "I won't say goodbye. I know we'll meet again."

"I hope so." He took both her hands in his one. "It'll be a fine day when it happens."

She turned away. Brister had everything ready. The duke shook hands, the duchess kissed him on the cheek. Reiner arose to convey them to the station.

They said their goodbyes to Coco and Crocker and

straggled to the door. Caroline turned for one more glance. Then she was gone. Buchanan felt a twinge of regret, a slight emptiness.

Mme. Velvet asked, "Have you had breakfast?"

"I'm starvin'," he told her.

They went to the dining room. She sat between Coco and Buchanan. Her eyes were bright; she was relaxed yet excited. As the food came and Buchanan began to eat as only he could, she laughed and applauded. "I love to see a big man eat. You might not believe it, but I can cook up a storm myself."

"I believe," said Buchanan.

"I've got to get to Denver. Bigby's a good man but the club needs me. How about you?"

"We got no more business here."

"You both need a rest. I've got rooms to spare."

"Uh-huh." He finished his coffee. "One thing. I want to see the Cutlers."

She said, "I'll be waitin'."

Coco followed him. They walked down the street to the jailhouse. The marshal admitted them. Cal Cutler lay bandaged, staring up at them.

Buchanan said, "You got your points, Cutler. You want some word sent to Essie Lou?"

"You know about her. . . . Oh, the papers I lost."

"Uh-huh."

"Gave me plumb away, did they?"

"Just about."

"Essie Lou." He hesitated. "No. Let her hate me when she finds out about us. Better that way."

Buchanan said, "Guess you're right. You know what? You should've thought about startin' over with her in the West instead of thinkin' on that other stuff. The South ain't goin' to rise again, Cutler. It's a waste and I'm sorry for you. I truly am."

Cutler said, "The hell with that, Buchanan. The South will conquer. We're just a sample. Don't feel sorry for us. We did what we could. You beat us. Damn Yankee."

He turned his head away.

Buchanan said, "I'm no Yankee. I'm an American. I'm a Westerner. And I don't figure to fight unless I got to. Goodbye, Cutler."

Reiner was back at the hotel. They sat together in the bar. Mme. Velvet joined them, linking arms with Buchanan.

Reiner said glumly, "Caroline's gone."

"You can't win 'em all," said Buchanan.

"She preferred you." Reiner looked at Mme. Velvet and sighed. "At least you got someone."

Mme. Velvet said sharply, "A hell of a lot more than 'someone,' mister. Believe it."

"I believe it, I believe it."

Buchanan said, "Whatever comes along, we take it as best we can. I won't be around when they hang the Cutlers. I wouldn't like it too much. You been a good man, Reiner. I do thank you for everything."

"You're welcome." He finished his drink. "When it's time for your train I'll be here."

"Thanks again."

Mme. Velvet said, "We'll be upstairs . . . restin'."

Coco said, "I been tellin' him. Women."

Buchanan paid no heed. He was, after all, wearier than he ever remembered. He allowed the little woman to steer him up the stairs. It had been his biggest fight. He was glad it was over. For once he felt like being pampered.

NEW FROM POPULAR LIBRARY